W9-BFD-691
3 0020 00014 2506

LOVE LOCKED IN

Dutton Books by Barbara Cartland

Love Locked In

The Wild, Unwilling Wife

Barbara Cartland

LOVE LOCKED IN

E. P. DUTTON
New York

Library of Congress Cataloging in Publication Data

Cartland, Barbara, 1902-
Love locked in.

I. Title.
PZ3.C247Ls3 [PR6005.A765] 823'.9'12 76-57985
ISBN: 0-525-14910-4

Published simultaneously in Canada by
Clarke, Irwin & Company Limited,
Toronto and Vancouver

10 9 8 7 6 5 4 3 2 1

First Edition

LOVE
LOCKED IN

Chapter One
1832

The *Duchesse* de Savigne lifted her eyes to her cousin, His Eminence Cardinal Xavier de Rochechant, sitting on the other side of the hearth, and asked in a voice that trembled:

"What has Aristide been . . . doing now?"

"That is what I came to talk to you about, my dear," the Cardinal replied.

"I guessed it!" the *Duchesse* said in a low voice. "I knew that you had not come all this way from Paris just to see me."

The Cardinal smiled.

"That sounds very ungallant," he replied. "As you know, Louise, I am always anxious to see you when I can spare the time, but I considered that my visit here today, for a very different reason, was urgent."

The *Duchesse* clasped her blue-veined hands, on which her rings seemed almost too heavy.

"Tell me the truth, Xavier," she said. "In what new scandal is Aristide involved?"

"You really want the truth?" the Cardinal asked.

"I know you intend to reveal it whatever my wishes may be," the *Duchesse* said with a flash of humour, "so I would like to hear it without your pretty phrases and without your trying to spare my feelings."

The Cardinal hesitated for a moment before he said almost harshly:

"Aristide is defaming the name of Savigne and making it a by-word for every outrage, scandal, and vice."

The *Duchesse* gave a little gasp, although it was what she had expected to hear, and there was a suspicion of tears in her eyes when she said in a voice her cousin could hardly hear:

"Tell me . . . everything."

She had been a very beautiful woman, but constant illness had left her face deeply lined and her skin pale to the point of transparency.

She was so thin that she looked as if a puff of wind would blow her away, and in fact the Cardinal had been surprised and shocked by her appearance when he arrived at the Château.

He had considered it his duty to come from Paris for the express purpose of asking the *Duchesse*'s help.

No-one knew better than he the damage which aristocrats like the *Duc* de Savigne were doing to the country at this particular moment in French history, by their wild extravagance and their exotic parties, which caused growing resentment.

"The White Terror" after Waterloo had been insignificant in comparison with the Red Revolution only twenty-three years earlier, in 1792. But the rebellion which had taken place only two years ago, in 1830, had made the whole country apprehensive.

In protest against the illiberal and reactionary role of Charles X, rioting had broken out in Paris, the Stock Exchange was set on fire, and the Arsenal and the powder deposit at Salpêtrière fell into the insurgents' hands. The Louvre and the Tuileries were taken.

Troops marched into the rebel districts, but they

were powerless in the narrow streets where the people threw furniture on their heads.

Six thousand barricades turned most of Paris into an entrenched camp; King Charles X was forced to abdicate and the *Duc* d'Orléans, Louis-Philippe, a descendant of Louis XIV, was invited to take his place and restore order.

This depended a great deal on regaining the confidence of the people, and the attitude and behaviour of members of the *ancien régime* like the *Duc* de Savigne were making it far harder than it would have been otherwise.

The *Duchesse* was waiting and after a moment the Cardinal said:

"It is not only the orgies which Aristide gives or takes part in every evening, it is the mistresses whom he flaunts through the streets of Paris and the stories of the extravagant presents he gives them which makes those who are living near to starvation restless, to say the least of it."

"You are afraid of a recurrence of violence?" the *Duchesse* asked quickly.

"There is always the chance that it will break out again," the Cardinal replied, "and I consider that to prevent such an explosion it is essential that the nobles who have returned to their Castles, their lands, and their rightful places in Society should set an example to those who have suffered so bitterly in the last sixteen years."

"You are right, Xavier," the *Duchesse* said. "Of course you are right. Have you spoken to Aristide about this?"

The Cardinal gave a little laugh with no humour in it.

"My dear Louise, do you imagine that he would listen to me? He has said often enough, and publicly, that religion is out-of-date. If he has attended Mass in the last ten years I have not heard of it."

The *Duchesse* put her hands up to her face and they were trembling.

"How could this have . . . happened to my . . . son of all . . . people?" she asked almost beneath her breath.

"I suppose it all stems from that regrettable episode in his life," the Cardinal said.

The *Duchesse* did not reply. They were both thinking of the tragedy which had overshadowed Aristide's youth and turned him from a charming, happy young man into a cynic who had gradually become the bitter reactionary he was now.

"There has been scandal after scandal," the Cardinal said after a moment. "Two weeks ago a young woman, well known in theatrical circles, although I would hesitate to call her an actress, tried to commit suicide."

The *Duchesse* gave an exclamation of horror, but he continued:

"She made a confession that was printed in every newspaper alleging that the cause of her unhappiness was Aristide's callous behaviour towards her."

"She had been his mistress?" the *Duchesse* asked.

"One of a dozen others," the Cardinal replied. "He apparently had dismissed her in a somewhat cruel fashion, and she decided, God help her, that life was not worth living without him."

"Women . . . always women!" the *Duchesse* murmured.

The Cardinal was silent for a moment, then he said:

"Aristide is now thirty. It is time he married and produced an heir."

The *Duchesse* looked at him in a startled fashion as His Eminence continued:

"You know as well as I do, Louise, that if there is no direct heir, the title and the Estates will go to that elderly cousin who lives in Montmartre with the artists, and has announced quite openly that he is a Republican and disapproves not only of titles, but also of personal possessions."

The *Duchesse* gave a little groan and the Cardinal finished:

"Heaven knows what will happen to the Estates if he inherits."

"Does Aristide know this?"

"Of course he knows it!" the Cardinal replied. "But quite frankly, he does not care!"

His voice sharpened as he continued:

"I do not think he cares for anything these days, not even the women whom he takes up on an impulse, and apparently without any consideration for their feelings, discards them as soon as they bore him."

The Cardinal's lips tightened as he finished:

"And Aristide is very quickly bored!"

"How could we . . . persuade him to be married? And even if he agreed, would it do any . . . good?"

"I have no idea," the Cardinal answered. "Frankly, I only feel it might be a solution and it might keep him away from Paris. It is the notoriety that he attracts which is doing so much harm. He is news, Louise, and you know what that means in the 'Gutter Press.' "

The *Duchesse* gave a deep sigh.

"I have prayed that Aristide would marry and give me a grandson," she said, "or rather many grandchildren. I have always regretted that I was able to have only one child."

"At least Léon died happy, knowing he had a son," the Cardinal said consolingly.

"He would hardly be happy if he could see him now," the *Duchesse* replied.

"That is why, Louise, we have to do something."

"You will speak to him on the subject of marriage?"

The Cardinal shook his head.

"No, Louise, you must do that."

He rose from the high-backed chair in which he had

been sitting to walk across the room towards the window.

As he moved in his red robes over the exquisite Savonnerie carpet, the sunshine coming through the window illuminated the priceless treasures with which the Château was furnished.

By some miracle the Château Savigne had been spared much of the devastation of the Terror of 1793.

Unlike the other Châteaux in the vicinity, it had been spared severe looting, and the present *Duc*'s grandfather had been far-seeing enough to remove most of the priceless treasures that had been handed down from generation to generation to a safe place where the Revolutionaries never found them.

Now they had been restored and the Château was, the Cardinal thought, one of the finest in the whole of France.

He may have been prejudiced, but he loved the Château Savigne, having known it since he was a young man when his beautiful cousin, Louise, had married the reigning *Duc*.

He looked out now on the great Park, with the spotted deer roaming beneath the trees, and in the distance he could see the faint silver of the Loire as it wound its way through the countryside.

There were great Châteaux on both sides of the river and many others in the vicinity.

When during the fifteenth century Charles VII had been expelled by the English from Paris, he spent the greater part of his time in Tours and in the Castles of the surrounding district.

His love for the province of Touraine was shared by most of his successors on the throne, during the two subsequent centuries.

The frequent presence of the King in the Loire Valley compelled the noblemen at Court to follow the Royal example.

For this reason an extraordinary number of Châteaux

clustered round the banks of the river and its tributaries.

Huge majestic Castles were erected by the competitive desire of each nobleman to build a larger and more magnificent house than his neighbour.

Many of the Châteaux had begun their history as medieval fortresses, but with the coming of the Renaissance they were developed into masterpieces of contemporary architecture, ornate and beautiful, which made all who saw them feel amazed at the wonders to be found in that part of France.

Now the owners who had fled at the time of the Revolution had returned to set their houses in order, many having the difficult task of completely refurnishing huge, empty, looted rooms.

But whatever effort they must make, the Cardinal thought, it was worth it, and if they could take so much trouble, why could not the *Duc* de Savigne follow their example?

He realised the *Duchesse* was waiting and he walked back from the window to say:

"There is only one person, Louise, who could make Aristide understand what is required of him, and that is you!"

"But how? Why should he listen to me? He has not done so for many more years than I care to remember."

"I have a feeling, although I may be wrong," the Cardinal said slowly, "that he is still fond of you in his own fashion. If he thought you were dying, Louise, it might bring him to his senses."

"Dying!" the *Duchesse* ejaculated.

Her eyes met the Cardinal's and after a moment he drew his chair nearer to her and sat down.

"Now listen to me, Louise . . ." he began.

* * *

The party, which had started quite conventionally, was growing very wild.

The superb dinner for fifty people had made the guests extremely gay and noisy, with both sexes flushed and excitable.

The ladies had not left the table and now it was obvious that they were becoming more abandoned—their flirtatious attitudes having given way to a voluptuous enticement which their partners apparently found irresistible.

At the head of the table, seated in his high-backed chair carved with his Coat-of-Arms, the *Duc* de Savigne leant back, watching those he was entertaining with an enigmatic expression on his face that was hard to read.

Those who knew him well often wondered how he managed, when he was enjoying himself, to appear in some curious way of his own so aloof and uninterested in everything that was proceeding round him.

On each side of him two beautiful women, both notorious for their charms, whispered in his ear, showing as they did so an inordinate amount of bare bosom.

The laughter was growing louder until it was superceded by music from the Gallery which overhung the far end of the Banqueting Hall.

The *Duc*'s Mansion in Paris was one of the largest and most impressive houses in the Champs Élysées.

Few people passed it without staring curiously at its ornate gold-tipped railings and wondering what was taking place in the vast rooms, which were described almost daily by reporters who apparently haunted the house in search of a spicy "tit-bit" for their newspapers.

Tonight's party, as more than one nobleman present thought uncomfortably, would undoubtedly be described in detail in *Le Figaro* and *Le Temps*.

Several of them hoped fervently that their names would not be mentioned; at the same time, it was hard to know these days who was in the pay of the Press.

For all they knew, the person who reported this evening's excesses might be one of their own blood, or certainly one of their own kind.

"I have something to tell you, *Monsieur le Duc,*" the woman on the *Duc*'s right hand said with pouting lips. "It is wickedly cruel, but it will make you laugh."

"I am waiting," the *Duc* said languidly.

"Do not listen to her," the woman on the other side interposed. "What she is going to tell you is something about me, and I swear to you it is not true. Promise you will not believe her!"

"How can I promise if I have not heard what she has to say?" the *Duc* asked.

"I assure you it is not credible, and what Aimie does not know she invents!"

"You must let me be the judge," the *Duc* said.

"Why not?" Rosette asked. "I trust you to find me innocent."

She looked at him provocatively as she spoke and the *Duc* smiled cynically.

"I doubt if anyone could do that, Rosette!" he replied. "Nevertheless I am prepared to learn about this wicked thing you are alleged to have done."

"I will tell you," Aimie said with satisfaction.

She bent forward to whisper in his ear and as she did so the music charmed several of the *Duc*'s guests into rising from the table to move onto the polished floor at the end of the room.

The dancing, if that was what it was called, was outrageous, and was more suitable to a disreputable Dance Hall than to the exclusive neighbourhood of the Champs Élysées.

Except for those indulging in such exuberance, the rest of the guests were too concerned with themselves to be interested, and now the women's gowns were slipping from their white shoulders and the men were unbuttoning their waist-coats.

Servants, as if at some previous command, were extinguishing the lights in the chandeliers, leaving only the candles in the sconces and those in the candelabra on the table to light the scene.

It was then that the two women whispering so intimately to the *Duc* were disturbed by another flamboyant, flashing-eyed, dark-haired beauty who had electrified Paris by her appearance at the Théâtre des Variétés.

She had arrived late at the party after her performance was over, and because dinner had started without her she had been forced to take a place not at the *Duc*'s side, as she expected, but further down the table.

Now she came up to him and he knew by the expression in her flashing eyes that she was ready to do battle with any rival for his affections.

"Monsieur!" she cried in the tone of a cooing dove but with an undercurrent of steel, "you are neglecting me!"

"I could never do that for long, Susanne," the *Duc* replied.

"Then turn *cette canaille* away and give me your attention," Susanne replied.

Aimie and Rosette looked at her angrily and she went on:

"Have they anything to offer you—you who seek perfection and boast that you are a connoisseur?"

The *Duc* looked amused but he did not answer.

"If it were a question of the judgement of Paris," she said, "there would, I know, be no doubt to whom you would award the golden apple."

"That may be your opinion, Susanne," Aimie said sharply, "but it is not ours!"

Susanne looked her up and down scornfully.

"You are intruding, Susanne," Rosette said. "We

are entertaining *Monsieur* and it is not very amusing for him or for us to listen to you crowing about yourself like a cock on a dung-hill."

Susanne struck an attitude which was dramatic and at the same time aggressive. She looked at the *Duc* and the expression in her eyes challenged him.

"It is up to you, *Monsieur,*" she said softly, and there was an invitation even in the movement of her lips.

Both Aimie and Rosette looked at him too and now there was no mistaking that all three women were waiting breathlessly for his verdict.

"If my knowledge of mythology is not at fault," the *Duc* said slowly after a moment, "when Paris was asked to judge between the goddesses they did in fact exhibit *all* their charms."

There was a moment's pause, then Susanne with a little laugh slipped her gown from her shoulders and after a moment both Aimie and Rosette followed her example.

The *Duc* made no movement, only after a moment he asked lazily:

"And the golden apple means . . . ?"

"Of course, it is to spend the night with you, *Monsieur,*" Susanne said.

Again there was a pause as the *Duc* looked at the three women standing in front of him, each proudly confident she would be the woman.

There was in fact little to choose between them; perhaps Susanne's waist was smaller, but her thighs were thicker than Rosette's, while Aimie's breasts were fuller.

At last the *Duc* said, his voice still languid but with a touch of amusement in it:

"The only diplomatic decision I can make is to divide the prize of myself in equal parts. Fortunately my bed is large enough!"

There was a shriek of astonishment, but it was obvious that the ladies accepted the suggestion without reserve.

The *Duc* glanced at his guests and realised that what the newspapers would undoubtedly declaim as "an exotic orgy, reminiscent of Roman times" was now taking place.

Raising her fallen garments and holding them across her breasts, Susanne bent towards him.

"Why are we waiting?" she asked.

The *Duc* met her glance and replied with a twist of his lips:

"You are impatient, Susanne, but then you have always been the same."

"I am impatient for you," she answered. "I am quite prepared to show these little rats from the sewers that they are both stupid and ignorant in *'les sciences galantes.'* "

The *Duc* was about to reply when a powdered flunkey dressed in the scarlet and gold Savigne livery stood at his side.

"This has arrived by special courier, *Monsieur le Duc*," he said, and held out a silver salver on which lay a letter.

The *Duc* looked at it indifferently and seemed about to wave the man away until the flunkey added:

"The man came from the Château Savigne, *Monsieur le Duc*."

The *Duc* sat up in his chair and took the letter from the salver.

He opened it, read what was written, and rose to his feet.

Without a word to the three women who were awaiting his commands, without even looking at them, he turned and walked from the room, followed by his servant.

* * *

His Eminence Cardinal de Rochechant, as he drove along the rough roads, thought as he had thought so often before that there was nothing more beautiful than what was known as the "Garden of France."

It was not only the Châteaux which were so impressive, but the Atlantic breezes penetrated as far as Tours, which was about two hundred kilometres from the sea, and created conditions of life rarely found so far inland.

Because of the configuration of the valley, wide and fertile, it had also been called the "Smile of France," the smile reminiscent of that on the face of the *Mona Lisa.*

This name had reason, since Leonardo da Vinci spent his last two years in the valley of the Loire in a small Château close to Amboise.

Since then more romance had in the course of centuries taken place on the banks of the Loire than of any other river in the world.

Soon, the Cardinal reflected, the dry months of the summer would divide the waters into many little streams which would flow green and pellucid among the yellow sand-banks and narrow islands.

They would be covered with the tangles of the olive-green willow which always thrived in this watery soil.

The small vineyards on the gentle slopes of the valley produced the delectable light wines which the Cardinal found he enjoyed more than any of the more full-bodied wines from other districts.

But as it happened he was at the moment not concerned with the beauty of the Loire Valley, which always moved him, but with the news he had received this morning.

It had arrived at the Château Blois, where he was staying, having deliberately delayed his return to Paris until the information he required came from the *Duchesse.*

Blois had been at one time a Royal residence, and the Cardinal was very comfortable there but he found it difficult to think of anything except the drama which he was aware was taking place at Château Savigne.

Almost clairvoyantly he imagined that the *Duc* on receiving his mother's letter had set off from Paris with all possible speed to go to her side.

The *Duchesse* had in fact written exactly the letter the Cardinal had suggested to her:

May 12, 1852. Château Savigne.

My Dearest Son,

I am in ill health and I feel I am not long for this World. I beg you to Visit me as soon as it is Possible, for I could not bear to Die without seeing Your dear Face once again, and hearing your Voice.

If it is inconvenient for You to leave Paris at this moment, You must forgive Me, but my Heart yearns for You and I shall pray that God will let Me remain in this World long enough to hold You in my arms before He takes me into His care.

I remain, my Dearest and most beloved Aristide,

Your Loving Mother,
Louise de Savigne.

The *Duc* did not wait for his carriage or for the innumerable retinue of valets and other personal servants with whom he always travelled in a state that was almost like a Royal progress.

Instead, accompanied only by his Comptroller and two grooms, he left Paris as dawn was breaking and set off across country towards Tours.

The *Duc*'s Comptroller was in fact a personal friend, one of the few he admitted to such intimacy.

Pierre de Bethune was the impoverished younger son of a nobleman who had lost his life and everything he possessed during the Revolution.

The *Duc* had found Pierre, whom he had known as a boy, eking out a precarious existence in the more sordid night-spots of Paris and had offered him a post in his household.

Pierre had rewarded him with a devotion which surprised other men of the *Duc*'s acquaintance and became in fact not only his constant companion but also his confidant.

They rode swiftly and without speaking for some time. Then Pierre turning to his employer said with a smile:

"This sweeps away the cob-webs, does it not, *Monsieur?*"

"That was what I was thinking," the *Duc* replied.

Dawn was rising, turning the countryside to gold, and if the *Duc* found it different from the usual debris of a dissolute evening or an untidy bed-room strewn with female garments, he did not say so.

His Comptroller merely thought that some of the lines of dissipation marked on his master's face were lightening. It might have been the effect of the dawn but he did not look so bored or so cynical.

"You realise, *Monsieur,*" Pierre de Bethune said, "that this will be the first time I have visited the Château Savigne?"

"The first time?" the *Duc* mused. "Well, I wonder what you will think of it—a great barrack of a place, although I think it has a certain charm."

He did not elaborate on what this was, and having ridden hard all day they slept the night in a small uncomfortable Hostel. Over an indifferent dinner, although the wine was good, Pierre de Bethune started to talk of the Château.

"Why do you so seldom go there, *Monsieur?*" he enquired.

"I should have thought that was obvious," the *Duc* replied uncompromisingly. "It bores me!"

"I am surprised at that," Pierre said. "You love

riding, and who can ride in real comfort in Paris? And I feel, although you have never said so, that you are fond of the country."

"It is dull, I tell you," the *Duc* said almost sharply. "Deadly dull! And as you know, Pierre, the one thing I try to avoid is boredom."

"Tell me about your home."

"What do you want to know?" the *Duc* enquired. "That it has turrets and towers—that it is in such a sheltered position that palm trees grow in the garden—that Louis XVI slept there and his bed-room, which I use, is unchanged?"

"It sounds fascinating," Pierre said, "and I suspect, although you will not admit it, that you loved it when you were young."

For a moment the *Duc* seemed to be very still, then he said:

"It is so long ago that I have forgotten."

But Pierre de Bethune knew that he lied.

They arrived at Savigne early in the morning and the *Duc* had been right, Pierre thought, in describing his house as having towers and turrets.

Never had he seen anything so attractive or so fairy-like as the great Château with its gardens sloping down to the banks of the river and its roofs and chimneys silhouetted against the blue sky.

The *Duc* rode up to the front door where the grooms were waiting to take his horse and then he walked up the broad steps through the line of bowing servants.

"May I welcome you, *Monsieur le Duc?"* the Clerk of Chambers asked.

"Take me to *Madame la Duchesse*," the *Duc* replied.

The Clerk of Chambers went ahead of him up the curving carved staircase and along the broad corridor to the South Wing, occupied by his mother ever since she had been widowed.

A maid opened the door, dropping a respectful

curtsey, and the *Duc* strode in, pulling off his gloves as he did so.

The *Duchesse* was lying in a huge canopied bed.

She looked very frail amongst the lace-edged pillows and the ermine cover was no whiter than the pallor of her face.

"My son!"

She held out her hands to him and the *Duc* took them in both of his, kissing them gently.

Like the Cardinal, he was in fact shocked by the difference in her appearance since he had last seen her: she seemed to have become almost disembodied and already part of the spiritual world.

"I came the moment I received your letter, Mama."

"Thank you . . . my dearest," the *Duchesse* said. "I have been praying that you would be . . . in time."

"You have seen the best doctors? Is there nothing they can do for you?"

"Nothing, dearest, and do not grieve for me. I shall be with your father, as I have longed to be ever since he left me."

The *Duc*'s fingers tightened on hers.

The maid closed the door and they were alone in the room.

"There is one thing I would . . . ask of you," the *Duchesse* said in a low voice, "just one thing . . . Aristide . . . before I . . . die."

"What is it, Mama?"

There was an expression in the *Duc*'s eyes which told her that he almost anticipated what she had to say.

"I cannot die in . . . peace unless I know that the . . . succession is . . . assured."

The *Duc* drew in his breath.

"It is time that you married, my beloved son," the *Duchesse* said, "and I want more than I have ever wanted anything in my whole life to hold . . . your son in my arms."

"It is impossible, Mama!"

"But why?" the *Duchesse* asked.

He did not reply and after a moment she said brokenly:

"Oh, Aristide, you were such a sweet and charming little boy and we loved you deeply . . . your father and I."

Her fingers tightened on his as she went on:

"When you grew older we were so proud of you. You had every talent, and you were so strong and athletic, which delighted your father."

The *Duc* moved a little restlessly.

"Then you changed. The son we knew and loved went away from me. I have thanked God many times that your father is not here to see the alteration."

"There is nothing that can be done about it, Mama. I am as I am, and as far as I am concerned I am content."

"Is that really true?" the *Duchesse* asked.

She looked as she spoke at the lines on his face, which seemed to be those of discontent, already etched from his nose to his mouth, and the dark blue shadows of dissipation under his eyes.

Once, the *Duchesse* thought despairingly, he had been the best-looking young man anyone could find in the whole length and breadth of France.

Now he appeared older than his years and he looked like a man who had drunk of the very dregs of life and found them sour.

"Please . . . Aristide," she said almost beneath her breath.

He rose from the side of her bed to walk away across the room.

On the opposite wall were a number of miniatures, all exquisitely painted, of the *Ducs* of Savigne down the ages.

They were a handsome lot, ending with his father, whose features were very like his own, except that there was a nobility about his expression that was inescapable.

He stood there with his back to the bed, and after a moment the *Duchesse* could no longer look at him.

She knew that she had failed and shut her eyes. The Cardinal had been wrong. Aristide no longer cared for her. They had not even the natural affection of mother and son left between them.

"I want to die," she told herself, "and there is no pretence about that. I shall die because I have nothing left to live for."

She had known all through the pain and discomfort she suffered especially in the winter that the one thing which kept her going was the thought that one day her son would come back to her.

One day he would live at the Castle and the empty corridors would come alive, the great rooms would be filled with the sound of voices and the laughter of children.

But now she knew that was only a dream, a dream that would never materialise; it was something she had merely conjured up, the sick fancy of an ill woman.

The *Duc* had finished his inspection of the family portraits.

They gleamed against the blue damask walls, their exquisitely jewelled frames glittering in the sunshine.

He walked back towards the bed and stood looking down at his mother.

She did not open her eyes, and because she was so still he had a sudden fear that she was no longer breathing.

"Mama!"

It was a call—an urgent call—and despondently she opened her eyes.

"I will do as you ask!"

"Aristide! Do you mean . . . that?"

"If it will make you happy."

"You know it will make me happier than I can ever tell you."

"Then it will be worth all the boredom and depression which it will bring me."

"Thank you, my darling. Now I have something to live for, although I do not think I shall linger long."

"You will have to live," the *Duc* said, "because this is your idea and I leave it entirely in your hands."

The *Duchesse* looked startled.

"You mean—?" she began.

"I mean," the *Duc* interrupted, "that I will personally take no initiative. Choose my wife yourself. I am sure she will prove very suitable. Arrange the marriage. It will have to be here in our own Chapel so that you can see me suitably shacked in Holy bedlock. You would not be well enough to travel elsewhere."

"But, Aristide—!"

"Those are my conditions," the *Duc* said. "I do not wish to see the girl or have anything to do with her until she is my wife. Then I will come here from Paris and stay long enough to breed the grandson you so fervently desire."

"But, dearest—" the *Duchesse* said again.

"I do not intend to argue about it," the *Duc* stated. "You have gained your way, Mama, and I have a suspicion that you were quite certain you would do so. Be content!"

The *Duchesse* put out her hands to touch his.

"I want you to be . . . happy," she said in a low voice.

The *Duc*'s lips twisted.

"Is that why you brought me here?"

"That is what I believe marriage will give you. I was, as you know, very happy with your father, and he with me."

"But I am not my father and never will be," the Duc said, "and you are very unlikely to find me a wife as charming and as beautiful as you, Mama."

"I shall try, my dearest, I shall try. But it will be difficult if you will not help me and make yourself pleasant."

"I dare say my wife, when I have one, will not find me unpleasant," the *Duc* said mockingly. "There are quite a number of women who appear to enjoy my company."

"What sort of women?" the *Duchesse* asked gently.

The *Duc* raised her hand to his lips.

"We have struck a bargain, Mama, you and I, and I have no wish to discuss it further. Now, if you will forgive me, I wish to bathe and change my clothes."

"I am deeply grateful for your coming when I wanted you," the *Duchesse* said.

"I have a feeling, Mama, that you are stronger than you appear. Your will-power at any rate has not diminished in its strength and determination!"

The *Duchesse*'s fingers tightened on his.

"I only want your happiness," she murmured again.

"I wonder what that elusive condition is really like?" the *Duc* asked. "Somehow I do not seem to have encountered it for so long that I have forgotten how to recognize it."

"Oh, Aristide—!"

There was a little throb in the *Duchesse*'s voice and the *Duc* said quickly:

"We are becoming absurdly sentimental! Make your plans, Mama, and as I have already promised, I will acquiesce in them. Do not let us bore ourselves by discussing them further."

He rose as he spoke.

For a moment he looked down at her, then he bent forward and kissed her on the cheek.

"Keep alive, Mama," he said quietly. "I have a feeling that Savigne will crumble into ruins without you being here."

He walked from the room, and having watched him

go the *Duchesse* lay back against her pillows feeling suddenly exhausted.

The Cardinal had been right, she thought. Aristide did still care for her, and because she had asked it of him he had agreed to be married.

It was a swifter victory than she had hoped for and at the same time she was apprehensive.

What woman would find him a congenial husband in the mood he was in now?

The *Duchesse* had not missed the underlying bitterness, the irony, and the cynicism in his voice when he promised to do what she wished.

Then she told herself that all that really mattered was that there should be an heir.

She faced the fact that Aristide, once the honeymoon—if it could be so called—was over, would doubtless return to the life he enjoyed in Paris.

She doubted, however optimistic the Cardinal might be, that a wife, or even a family, would change him back into a respectable land-owner directing his country possessions as the King and the new Régime thought so desirable.

At the same time, the first step had been taken. Aristide had agreed to be married and now the question was to find him a suitable wife.

The *Duchesse* reached out her hand for the little gold bell which stood by her bed-side.

Almost immediately the door was opened and one of her lady's-maids came into the room.

"My writing-paper, ink-pot, and pen," the *Duchesse* commanded. "Tell a groom to be ready to take a message immediately to His Eminence the Cardinal at Blois."

The maid curtseyed.

"I'll do that, *Madame*."

'The Cardinal will be delighted!' the *Duchesse* thought.

When he had suggested what she should say and

do, she had been almost sure that his optimism was unfounded and that Aristide would not respond.

But in fact he had come to Savigne at a moment's notice, riding all the way, and because he believed she might die he had surrendered his freedom without even a struggle.

"God help him . . . God help my son," the *Duchesse* prayed.

It was a prayer that she had repeated and repeated over the years, and she had begun to feel that God was not interested in her pleas and had turned away from her.

Now everything was changed, and as the maid returned with her writing materials she sat up in bed and took the white quill pen in her hand. . . .

* * *

In the carriage His Eminence the Cardinal opened the *Duchesse*'s letter and read it again.

He could hardly believe that Aristide had given his mother a completely free hand in choosing him a bride and that he would take no personal part in it. But there it was, clearly written in the *Duchesse*'s elegant hand-writing!

Now the Cardinal drew another piece of paper from the pocket of his crimson robes.

On it were jotted down the names that he and the *Duchesse* had discussed together as being suitable brides for the *Duc* de Savigne.

While he had been at the Château Blois the Cardinal had taken the opportunity of very discreetly sounding his host about the girls whose family names were written on the list he and the *Duchesse* had compiled.

He had chosen his words with care.

"Do you often see the *Duc* de Foucauld-Fleury?" he asked.

"He and his family frequently are here," was the answer.

"Does that mean he has a large family?"

"Yes, indeed, although most of them are married."

"Of course, I remember. His son made an excellent alliance. I believe I met his wife in Paris."

"There is only one of the *Duc*'s seven children who is still unwed."

"I think I heard somewhere that her name is—Isabelle," the Cardinal murmured a little vaguely.

"Your Eminence is right. An attractive girl. I am surprised she has not yet married, but apparently the young man to whom she was more or less affianced three years ago was regrettably killed in an accident."

"That was unfortunate," the Cardinal replied.

"Very, but I expect the *Duc* will be finding a husband for her soon."

The Cardinal changed the subject. He had found out what he wanted to know.

Later he questioned his host about the *Marquis* d'Urville and found that his daughter, Henriette, was just eighteen and noted as being a beauty.

There was only one other name on the list, but because both the Cardinal and the *Duchesse* were quite certain they would have to look no further than the *Duc*'s Castle or the *Marquis*'s Château to find a suitable bride, he ignored it.

"Whatever she is like," the Cardinal told himself, "it is unlikely the wretched girl will be able to hold the affections of Aristide for long."

He sighed.

"But at least he can offer her an ancient name written into the history of France, great possessions, and a Château without its peer in the whole district, even including Chambard and Chenenceaux."

They were near Chenenceaux at the moment and he leaned out of his carriage to look at the famous building which had belonged to the most beautiful woman France had ever known.

Diane de Poitiers had been twenty years older than Henry II, but he loved her until he died, and a contemporary wrote that when she was nearly sixty-seven she was as beautiful to look upon and as attractive as she had been at thirty.

Of course, the Cardinal reflected, the Count had implied that Diane used witch-craft to keep her loveliness, and it was reported that she took some special sort of broth every day which rendered her immune from the encroaches of time.

The Cardinal, however, a keen historian and a man of intelligence, had always thought that one of the reasons why Diane de Poitiers kept her looks until she was an old woman was the fact that she always bathed in cold water and never partook of the rich food and the profusion of wines which were to be found at the King's table.

He could see Chenenceaux now very clearly and the unusual manner in which it was built on two piers of a former mill resting on the bed of the Cher.

There was a two-storeyed gallery on the bridge over the river, and reflected in the still water it looked romantic and very beautiful.

"That," the Cardinal said to himself with a sudden unusual twist of imaginative fancy, "is how a woman should look, beautiful and at the same time excitingly original, with perhaps a touch of mystery and excitement about her so that a man would never be bored."

The word inevitably brought him back to the *Duc!*

He had the feeling that the woman who could divert the *Duc* from the excesses with which he relieved his *ennui* had not yet been born!

Chapter Two

His Eminence the Cardinal driving through the sunlit countryside was deep in thought.

He was wondering how he could explain to the *Duchesse* that he had failed in the quest on which she had sent him.

He had never imagined for a moment that he would not succeed in obtaining the consent of one of the young women she had chosen to become the bride of the *Duc* de Savigne.

He had thought the most suitable one would prove to be Isabelle, the daughter of the *Duc* de Foucauld-Fleury.

He had arrived at the *Duc*'s Castle, a huge barrack which could be exceedingly cold in winter, to be greeted enthusiastically by both the *Duc* and the *Duchesse,* who were devout Catholics.

"It is far too long, Your Eminence, since we have had the pleasure of welcoming you to this part of the country," the *Duc* said genially.

"My duties in Paris unfortunately keep me fully occupied," the Cardinal replied, "but I assure you, *Monsieur,* it is a very great pleasure for me to be in Touraine again."

"And it is certainly a pleasure for us," the *Duc* answered.

The Cardinal enjoyed an excellent luncheon and noted with satisfaction that Isabelle was an attractive young woman with, he was sure, a lot of common sense, and who was by no means untalented.

'She could certainly make Aristide a commendable wife,' he thought.

After luncheon the *Duc* took the Cardinal into his private Study, which was one of the most magnificent and impressive rooms in the Castle.

"I fancy, Your Eminence," he said, "that you have a special reason for calling on me. When I received your message from Blois I had the feeling, although I may be wrong, that it was not entirely for the pleasure of my company that you wished to come here."

The Cardinal smiled.

"You are very perceptive, *Monsieur le Duc,* and in fact you are right. I have an ulterior motive for my visit."

"I was sure of it," the *Duc* said, "although I have no idea what it can be."

The Cardinal paused for a moment before he said:

"I am empowered by the *Duchesse* de Savigne and by her son, the *Duc*, to suggest that a liaison between your two families might be to the mutual advantage of the young people concerned."

He was watching the *Duc* as he spoke and saw him stiffen. For a moment there was an almost incredulous look in his eyes.

Then, when he seemed to be feeling for words, the door opened and Isabelle came in.

"Forgive me, *mon Père,* if I interrupt you and His Eminence, but you left your spectacles in the Dining-Room and I thought you might need them."

She put them on a small table beside her father's chair.

He looked at her, then as she turned to leave the room he said:

"Wait, Isabelle! I was just about to tell His Eminence that I have agreed to your marriage with Michel de Croix, and that it will take place in the autumn."

For a moment Isabelle's eyes widened as if she could not believe what she was hearing. Then a look of radiance seemed to transform her face into unexpected beauty.

"Do you mean that, Papa?" she asked in a low voice.

"But of course!" the *Duc* replied. "As I was going to inform His Eminence, your mother and I are satisfied that Michel de Croix is exactly the husband with whom we feel you will be happy."

The Cardinal was a perceptive man. He knew quite well that the *Duc* had only made up his mind at this precise moment that his daughter should marry a man whose eligibility had been hotly contested until the suggestion of another alliance had decided the issue.

It was a blow he had not expected, but the Cardinal reacted like a trained diplomat.

He managed to congratulate Isabelle and give her his blessing on her coming nuptials with what passed for a note of sincerity in his voice.

"I must regret, Your Eminence," the *Duc* said when Isabelle had left the room, "that your journey has been for nothing."

"I would not say that," the Cardinal replied. "I have greatly enjoyed meeting you again, *Monsieur le Duc*, and I hope it will not be long before I have the pleasure of entertaining you in Paris."

"You are very gracious," the *Duc* replied.

Their eyes met and they understood each other. Both knew without expressing it in words exactly what had taken place.

As the Cardinal drove away and he metaphorically crossed the *Duc*'s daughter off his list, he wondered for the first time if his task might not be as easy as he and the *Duchesse* had anticipated.

He had assumed that the main hurdle would be to persuade the *Duc* to marry, but now it seemed, if the *Duc* de Foucauld-Fleury was anything to go by, that it might prove more difficult to find a bride.

The *Marquis* d'Urville made no pretence of hiding his real feelings, nor did he doll them up as the *Duc* had done with what the Cardinal told himself were "pretty ribbons."

"Allow Henriette to marry de Savigne!" he exclaimed. "Your Eminence must be deranged if you think for one moment that I would entrust any woman, let alone my daughter, to that lecher, that young swine who has made the name de Savigne a by-word in the gutters of Paris!"

The *Marquis* was a stout man and he grew so crimson in the face at the very idea that the Cardinal was afraid he might have a stroke.

"It was but a suggestion, my dear *Marquis*," he said soothingly.

"A suggestion which never should have been made to me," the *Marquis* stormed. "Does the *Duchesse* think that I am deaf? That I do not hear the stories that are told about her son? That I am blind so that I cannot read the newspapers?"

He paused for breath before he added:

"If you ask me, Your Eminence is wasting your time. No father worthy of the name would permit one of his daughters to enter the Château Savigne—let alone marry its owner! I personally would rather see my child dead!"

That was certainly plain speaking, the Cardinal told himself, as he drove away from the Château, and he envisaged that the *Viscomte* de Boulaincourt's answer might be the same, before he discovered on arrival that his daughter's engagement had been announced the previous week.

He would however have been very obtuse if he had not realised that the *Viscomte* was relieved that he was not put in the unpleasant position of having to refuse an alliance with the House of Savigne.

"I expect you left Paris, Your Eminence, before the notice of engagement appeared in several of the newspapers," he said. "It is in fact a marriage on which my wife and I set our hearts many years ago, and it is extremely satisfactory to realise that both my daughter and her fiancé are very much in love with each other."

Once again the Cardinal gave everyone concerned his blessing. Then he was driving away over the dusty roads, knowing that now he had nowhere to go but the Château Savigne to report the complete and utter failure of his mission.

"There must be other young ladies," he tried to tell himself optimistically.

Then he remembered that the *Duchesse* had gone very carefully over the list of eligible young women in the district.

Now the only thing to do, the Cardinal thought, was to go further afield, perhaps to the South of France, or the West or North, where the name Savigne would mean something different from what it meant in a province which was so near to Paris.

He only hoped that the *Duchesse* would not insist on his making the journey in person to visit such families.

He was not only extremely busy in Paris, he was also very comfortable there, and he found it tiring to be bumping over dusty roads and sleeping in unfamiliar beds.

'I should never have become involved in this,' he thought with a touch of irritability.

But then he knew that because he was related to the *Duchesse* and because he had been extremely fond of the last *Duc*, his conscience would not let him rest until he had tried by every means in his power to save their son from himself.

Because it came naturally to him he said a prayer that some way might be found to help a sinner who at least in God's sight would not be beyond redemption.

Then almost as if in direct answer to his prayer, he saw as the carriage drove by a sign-post at the corner of a road which read: "Monceau-sur-Indre 5 Kilometres."

The Cardinal put up his hand.

"Stop the carriage!" he commanded.

His Chaplain, sitting opposite him, an earnest young man, pale and somewhat cadaverous-looking from over-fasting, jerked to attention.

"Stop the carriage, *Monseigneur?*" he questioned in surprise.

"You heard what I said!" the Cardinal answered, and hastily the Chaplain obeyed the order.

The six horses were pulled to a standstill and one of the out-riders wearing the Cardinal's colourful livery came riding to the open window.

"You require something, Your Eminence?"

"Turn the horses round," the Cardinal ordered, "and take me to the Château Monceau. It is at the end of the village, beyond the Church."

"Very good, Your Eminence!"

With some difficulty the heavy carriage was turned a little way down the road and the cavalcade started back, turning down the narrow way towards the small village of Monceau.

The Cardinal had been right in saying that the Château was easy to find.

Just beyond the Church there was a pair of wrought-iron gates, sadly in need of paint, and a short drive where the trees had overgrown so that they formed a green tunnel whose branches occasionally swept the top of the carriage.

At the end of it was the Château with its pointed turrets and dormer windows.

Its Gothic symmetry was reflected in a small stream which at one side of the Château had broadened into a lake.

The trees had grown round the house until its grey stone was framed and almost enclosed by them.

Looking at it as they turned on the unkempt gravel sweep in front of the porticoed door, the Cardinal thought it looked even more like the Castle of "The Sleeping Beauty" than when he had last seen it.

Knowing they were not expected, the Chaplain looked at the Cardinal for instructions.

"Enquire if the *Comte* de Monceau is at home," he commanded, and the Chaplain alighted from the carriage just as the door was opened by an elderly servant.

The Chaplain returned.

"The servant said that the *Comte* is in his Library, Your Eminence, and he has gone to inform him of your arrival."

The Cardinal alighted and walked slowly up the steps.

Only as he reached the top of them did a man come hurrying through the Hall, both hands outstretched in welcome.

"Xavier!" he said. "This is a most delightful surprise!"

He reached the Cardinal's side, clasped both his hands, and then as if he suddenly remembered his rank, genuflected and kissed his ring.

"My dear Gérard," the Cardinal said. "I was passing the end of the road to the village and suddenly realised how long it was since we last saw each other."

"Come in! Come into the Library," the *Comte* said. "We will drink a glass of wine and you must tell me all that has happened to you since we last met."

"That will take time," the Cardinal replied with a smile.

"You will stay to dinner, or the night, if it pleases you?"

"I am expected at the Château Savigne; but dinner, if we could have it early, Gérard, would be most pleasant."

The *Comte* made a sound which was a wordless expression of joy, and, having shown the Cardinal into the Library, hurried to the door to give the order for the servant to bring wine.

He crossed the room to look at the Cardinal, who had seated himself on one of the few available chairs.

Everywhere else there were books.

Never had he thought it possible in all his experience to find so many books accumulated in one room, large though it was.

Not only were the walls covered with them, but there were great piles in every corner, on every table, on every chair, and it was obvious that before his arrival the *Comte* had been working at his desk.

It was strewn with manuscripts and also with books, some open, many of them with pieces of paper sticking out of their leaves to mark a special place.

When the *Comte* reached the Cardinal's side he looked up at him and said:

"Let me look at you, Gérard. You have certainly changed very little since the days when we enjoyed life together."

"It was a long time ago," the *Comte* remarked.

He was in fact a very handsome man, although untidily dressed, as if he found anything which kept him from his books irksome, and he looked far younger than his years.

There was very little grey in his hair, while the Cardinal's was almost white. His eyes sparkled when he talked and his lips smiled spontaneously.

"Tell me about yourself, Xavier," he said. "I know

how important you have become, and what a great power you are in Paris."

"I wish that were true," the Cardinal said with a sigh. "Few people today listen to the Church."

"I believe that is so," the *Comte* agreed, "but I always knew, Xavier, in those days when we were both students struggling to acquire knowledge, that you would reach the heights, while I . . ."

He made a gesture towards his desk.

"You have had a book published, I believe," the Cardinal said.

"Two, as it happens," the *Comte* replied, "but who reads them? People are not interested in the past. They are too busy living in the present."

"Nevertheless, whatever happens in the world, scholars and those who record history are a necessity for future generations," the Cardinal said quietly. "When I die I shall doubtless be forgotten, while you, Gérard, will be read perhaps many centuries ahead."

The *Comte* laughed and it was a boyish sound.

"You are just the same, Xavier, forever inspiring those who will listen to you. I shall always remember your first sermons in that dingy little Church in the slums of Montparnasse. You started out with—was it twelve in the congregation?—and ended up with being unable to get everyone inside the building!"

The Cardinal gave another sigh.

"It was hard work, Gérard, but I think sometimes I have never been so happy."

There was something in the way he spoke which made the *Comte* look at him sharply and say:

"You chose a hard road when you decided to renounce the usual blessings of mankind—a home, a wife, and children. I admired you for it then, Xavier, and I admire you now."

A servant came into the Library to set down a bottle of wine and two glasses.

He had difficulty in finding room on the table for

the salver on which they stood, but finally he compromised by putting it on top of several books.

The Cardinal noted with pleasure that it was one of the local wines for which he had a partiality, and when the glass was handed to him he sipped it appreciatively before he said:

"Tell me, Gérard, about yourself. I was sure that you would be happy in your marriage, although I could not attend the wedding."

"I quite understood that you were too busy to spare the time," the *Comte* said. "Do you realise, Xavier, that it is nearly twenty years since we have seen each other? And yet I remember so many things we used to talk about."

"As if it were yesterday," the Cardinal murmured as if to himself.

"I wish you had known Fleur," the *Comte* said. "She was not only beautiful but also very intelligent. She helped me with my books, she made my life a Paradise that is not granted to many men in this world."

"She is no longer with you?" The Cardinal asked.

"She died nearly three years ago," the *Comte* answered.

There was a note in his voice that told the Cardinal of the agony he must have passed through on losing her.

"I am deeply sorry," the Cardinal said. "And I am sorry too that I did not realise you had been bereaved. I would have gladly come to see you and tried to bring you a little comfort."

At the same time, he wondered if in fact he was telling the truth.

Would he really have left his many commitments in Paris and journeyed to Touraine just to succour a friend, even Gérard de Monceau, who had meant so much to him in his youth?

"There was nothing anyone could do," the *Comte* said, "and Syrilla was with me, thank God!"

"Syrilla?" the Cardinal questioned.

"My daughter," the *Comte* explained. "We did think when she was born that we might ask you to christen her, but already you had become famous, Xavier. You had already begun to move up the ladder towards your present position."

The *Comte* smiled before he added:

"We often talked of you, my wife and I. She was always interested in how much our friendship had meant to me when we were young. We quiet countryfolk could not presume to intrude into the world of affairs in which you play such a vital role."

"Tell me about Syrilla," the Cardinal suggested.

There was a sudden light in the *Comte*'s eyes as he said:

"She is lovely in mind, body and soul. I will show you a portrait of her which has recently been executed by a young artist who was spending his holiday in the village. He asked permission to paint Syrilla, and I think it is an excellent likeness."

He rose to walk across the Library to where in a far corner almost obscured by books the Cardinal could see there was an unframed canvas standing on a low easel.

The *Comte* had just picked it up in his hands when through the long window which opened into the garden there appeared a slender figure in a white gown.

The girl ran across the room, and as she did so the Cardinal thought she moved with an unusual grace.

It was almost as if she floated, her feet hardly touching the ground, her full skirts brushing against the piles of books as she passed them.

"Papa!" she said in a lilting voice which was also musical. "I have something so exciting to tell you!"

"What is it, my dearest?" the *Comte* asked.

"I was with Jacques in the Park while he was tend-ing the baby lambs which have just been born, when something quite extraordinary happened."

"What was it?" the *Comte* asked.

"One of them, when he picked it up from the grass, appeared to be dead, in fact I thought there was no hope for it. Then Jacques held it in his arms, opened its mouth, and blew into it! He blew hard, Papa, giving his breath, as it were, to the lamb, and you will hardly believe this but it came alive!"

"That certainly sounds extraordinary," the *Comte* agreed.

"It *was* extraordinary!" Syrilla said. "Do you think it possible that we ourselves can give life to those who need it?"

"Life comes from God," the Cardinal interposed, "but sometimes we have the privilege of transmitting it to others."

Syrilla started as he spoke and turned round to look at him, having had, he knew, no idea there was anyone else in the room except her father.

Now the Cardinal saw that she was very lovely, at the same time quite unlike anything he had expected.

For one thing she was fair. Her hair was golden and her eyes were very blue, and her skin was white with just a touch of colour on the cheeks.

She was small and exquisitely made and as she moved towards him he realised again that she had a grace that he had seldom seen in any young woman except perhaps a ballerina.

"This is my daughter, Syrilla, Xavier," the *Comte* said proudly.

Syrilla sank down in front of the Cardinal and kissed the great emerald ring he wore.

"Forgive me, Your Eminence," she said. "I had no idea that Papa had a visitor."

"I am an old friend," the Cardinal replied, "and it is very remiss of me that I did not know of your existence until a few moments ago."

Syrilla smiled and he noticed that she had a dimple on each side of her mouth.

"I know who you are," she said, "because Papa has so often spoken of you. What fun you must have had when you were students together!"

"We did indeed," the Cardinal replied, "and it is my loss that your father and I have almost lost touch with each other."

"Now you are here," Syrilla said softly, "may I look at your horses? For I feel such that Your Eminence will have arrived with a very impressive entourage."

"I am sure they will be delighted as I am to make your acquaintance," the Cardinal replied.

"Before you become so immersed in His Eminence's horse-flesh that you forget everything else," the *Comte* said, "will you tell Cook that His Eminence will be staying for dinner and she must do her best at such short notice. We must also dine early."

"You cannot stay the night?" Syrilla asked the Cardinal.

"I am afraid not," he replied, "but I shall look forward to dining with you and your father."

"It will be very exciting for us," Syrilla said, "but do not be disappointed with what you may find very simple fare."

She gave him a smile before she moved towards the door.

The Cardinal watched her go. Then as the door shut behind her he said to the *Comte:*

"How could you have fathered anything so exquisite? For the first time, Gérard, I think I am rather envious of you."

"She is lovely, is she not?" the *Comte* remarked, "and very like her mother."

As if knowing that the Cardinal wanted an explanation, he went on:

"Fleur came from Normandy and that of course accounts for Syrilla's fair hair and blue eyes. I have always said that she looks more English than French, but I assure you she is very much a Frenchwoman. Moreover, she cooks like one, so do not be afraid that you will not enjoy your dinner."

He paused before he said eagerly:

"Do you remember that dirty little restaurant we used to patronise on the Left Bank because it was cheap?"

"Of course I remember," the Cardinal answered.

"I have not thought of it again until this moment," the *Comte* went on. "But how amusing it was on Saturday nights when we used to talk and argue until the early hours of the morning."

"And the room was so thick with smoke that one could not see across it," the Cardinal added.

"I think it was those arguments which made me want to write," the *Comte* said.

They reminisced of the past for some time until the *Comte* glanced at the clock and said:

"I am sure you would like to wash before dinner."

He paused as if a thought struck him and said:

"Surely you are not traveling alone? Does not a Cardinal, like a Bishop, always have a Chaplain with him?"

"My Chaplain is continually worried about the lusts of the flesh," the Cardinal replied. "As a result, he fasts so that he looks as if I ill treat him, which I assure you I do not! Today is one of his total-fast days, so he will be quite content to sit in the carriage or walk about your grounds, and will not wish to join us."

"You are sure of that?" the *Comte* asked. "I would not wish to appear inhospitable."

"And I have no desire that Father Pagerie, who is, I regret to say, somewhat of a bore, should spoil the intimacy of our reunion dinner."

It was in fact a joyous meal.

The food was not only superlative but cooked, as

only a Frenchman could appreciate, in a manner that made it taste like ambrosia, while the wine, which came from the *Comte*'s small vineyard, was undoubtedly a nectar which would never survive being transported anywhere else.

There was not only good food, but also good conversation.

The two old friends vied with each other in relating incidents and anecdotes of their past which made both themselves and Syrilla laugh until the tears came into their eyes .

Syrilla found herself wishing that more of her father's old friends would visit them and entice him away from his books, which he could seldom be persuaded to leave even for an hour.

Watching her and listening to her, the Cardinal thought she was one of the most attractive and unusual young women he had ever met.

It was not only her beauty which was so striking, it was also, he thought, something spiritual in her face that he missed in other women, especially those he met in Paris.

If her laughter rang out untrammelled and occasionally she contributed to their conversation a sentence that was witty and gay, it struck exactly the right note.

He realised too that she was not only intelligent but, as might be expected of her father's daughter, extremely well educated.

He made a joke in Latin which she understood and capped with a Greek quotation in very much the same manner that her father had done when they had duelled together in words so many years ago.

Finally the Cardinal realised that time was getting on and he knew that he should give instructions for his carriage to be brought round from the stables to the front door.

And yet he was loath to leave.

This had been an interlude in his busy life which had

meant more to him than he could express in words.

It was only as he reached the Library that a sudden thought struck him.

"How old is Syrilla?" he asked the *Comte*.

"She was eighteen last January," he answered. "I am afraid she leads a very dull life here with me, but as you see she appears to be content, and no man could have a more loving or considerate daughter."

"And yet at eighteen she could certainly be thinking of marriage," the Cardinal said.

The *Comte* looked uneasy.

"I have of course considered it, Xavier, but we live such a secluded existence, Syrilla and I, that I am afraid we receive no invitations and give none. I suppose there are young men in the vicinity, but if there are we do not make their acquaintance."

The Cardinal considered for a moment.

He knew that if he obeyed his instinct he should say good-bye and leave this little oasis of peace undisturbed, and yet he thought that perhaps some Power greater than himself had guided him here for a special purpose.

How he could conceive such a thing he had no idea, because he knew that what he had to suggest was an outrage against decency, or rather against this exquisite creature who had obviously no knowledge of the world and its wickedness.

"I cannot do it!" he told himself.

Then he envisioned the *Duchesse*'s pleading face and was certain that she had not long to live.

How could he return to her, to all intents and purposes empty-handed?

He cleared his throat.

"You have not asked me, Gérard," he began, "how I happen to be in Touraine at this moment."

"I imagine it must be something very important to drag you away from Paris," the *Comte* replied.

"I consider it to be important that I should find a

bride for the *Duc* de Savigne," the Cardinal answered.

"Of the Château Savigne?" the *Comte* enquired. "It is a magnificent piece of architecture! As I expect you know, Xavier, it has great historical significance because in the Middle Ages . . ."

"I know the history of Savigne well," the Cardinal interrupted.

He knew that once the *Comte* became involved in historical reminiscences it would be difficult to bring him back to the point.

"What I am going to ask is whether you would consider a marriage between Syrilla and the *Duc*."

The *Comte* stared at him in astonishment and the Cardinal knew that the idea of such a match had never crossed his mind.

"You mean—he is the right age?"

"He is in fact a little over thirty," the Cardinal said, "and he bears a great name and owns great possessions."

He paused, then as if he could find nothing else to say about the *Duc* he added:

"Syrilla would make a beautiful *Duchesse*."

The *Comte* walked across the Library and back again before he answered:

"My wife and I often talked about what we would do when the time came for Syrilla to marry. I have not told you, Xavier, that Fleur was married before. She was a widow and she was in fact thirty-five before we met each other and fell in love at first sight."

There was an unmistakable pain in his voice before he said:

"That is why every year we spent together was so very precious to us both, and why when Syrilla was born it was a miracle for which we thanked God."

"I can understand that," the Cardinal said sympathetically.

"Fleur's first marriage was a very unhappy one. She was married when she was very young to a man much older than herself who was a brute and a bully. Because of the way she suffered, we always swore that never would we submit Syrilla to an arranged marriage."

The Cardinal's spirits dropped.

This was another disappointing answer to his proposition, he thought, and he told himself that he had not been really hopeful, even while he had made the suggestion.

The *Comte* de Monceau, while poor and of no particular social consequence because he was a recluse, was nevertheless in blood and breeding the equal of the Savignes.

It would not be a case of the *Duc* condescending to marry someone beneath him if he took Syrilla as his wife.

In fact the situation was, the Cardinal realised, that once again the bride's family was unwilling and he was no further on to finding a wife for the *Duc* of one of the oldest families in France.

"My wife and I planned that when the time came we would ask Syrilla whether or not she was willing to marry the man in question," the *Comte* was saying. "As you can imagine, Fleur had a horror of a *mariage de convenance.*

"Yes, I can understand that," the Cardinal said, "but as Syrilla has never met the *Duc* of Savigne there is hardly much point in asking you."

And there was no question, he thought, of her being able to meet the *Duc.*

The *Duchesse* had told him in her letter that Aristide had refused to meet his bride before he actually married her, and by this time he would have gone back to Paris to his disreputable companions and the excesses of behaviour which made the Cardinal feel sick when he thought about them.

"It is getting late," he said, "and I think, Gérard, I must be on my way."

"No—wait a moment!" the *Comte* exclaimed. "You have made me a proposition, and I think it only right and proper that as it concerns Syrilla she should hear what you have to say."

He smiled and there was a mischievous look in his eyes as he went on:

"After all, if nothing else, it will prove good practise for her in refusing the overtures of importunate young men! Now that you have put it into my head, I can see I must try to be a little less selfish and consider my daughter's future."

"I certainly think you should do that," the Cardinal said. "You may wish to live in the past, Gérard, but Syrilla has the present to think about. And she is very lovely."

"For once, Xavier, I accept your sermonising, and admit I have been in the wrong," the *Comte* replied. "I shall turn over a new leaf."

"Not of a book, I hope!" the Cardinal cried. "That would be fatal, for you would forget everything else but what is on the printed page."

They both laughed in the affectionate manner of old friends who had shared many jokes together.

The *Comte* than went to the door to open it and call for Syrilla.

She came running towards him saying:

"I feel sure you are going to tell me that His Eminence is ready to leave. I was just making sure that his coachmen and out-riders have been fed. His Chaplain has refused everything, food, drink, and even to smile at me!"

She walked into the Library as she was speaking and the Cardinal said:

"I cannot believe there are many men who do that."

"He looks very miserable," Syrilla said. "Can it be possible that Your Eminence is cruel to him?"

"He is cruel to himself," the Cardinal answered. "I

cannot help feeling that to him even laughter is one of the temptations of the devil."

"I hope not," Syrilla replied, "because if so we three will all spend a long time in Purgatory!"

She looked so lovely, smiling up at him with her eyes twinkling and the dimples showing on each side of her mouth, that once again the Cardinal had an impulse not to disturb the even tenor of her ways. But already it was too late.

"His Eminence has put a proposition to me, Syrilla," the *Comte* was saying, "which I think you ought to hear."

"What is it, Papa?"

"His Eminence has asked whether you would be prepared to accept the hand in marriage of the *Duc* de Savigne!"

As the *Comte* spoke the Cardinal hoped that Syrilla had never heard of the *Duc*, for he felt he could not bear to see her expression alter and become shocked or disdainful.

Worse still, that he would see in her eyes that disgust which he had felt when he learnt of some of the *Duc*'s more outrageous exploits.

But to his astonishment there was at first an expression of incredulity, then one of radiance mirrored in her eyes.

"The *Duc* de Savigne?" she asked in a low voice. "Do you really mean . . . the *Duc?*"

"You know he lives not far from here—at Château Savigne," the *Comte* said.

"I know. I went there once with Mama," Syrilla replied.

She looked enquiringly at the Cardinal.

"But . . . why should he be . . . interested in me?"

"The *Duc* wishes to marry," the Cardinal said. "It would make his mother happy and it would make me very happy, Syrilla, if you would consider him as your future husband."

As he spoke he hoped that God would forgive him, not only for what he was saying but also for even suggesting to this exquisite child that she could become the wife of Aristide de Savigne.

There was a pause and it seemed to the Cardinal that Syrilla's eyes grew larger and more radiant and an inner light seemed to glow from her that he could not understand.

Then, as both men waited, Syrilla said in a low voice which was very clear:

"I would be . . . honoured . . . deeply honoured and very . . . proud to be the wife of the *Duc* de Savigne!"

For a moment it was impossible for the Cardinal to speak.

He stared at Syrilla as if he could not have heard her aright. Then the *Comte* said:

"Do you mean what you are saying?"

"Yes, Papa."

"But you have never met the *Duc*."

"I have . . . seen him," Syrilla answered, "and I have thought of him very often."

The *Comte* stared at her in perplexity. Then he said a little uncertaintly:

"If that is—what you want."

It seemed to the Cardinal that he had difficulty in collecting his scattered senses.

"I know it will delight *Madame la Duchesse,* the *Duc*'s mother," he said to Syrilla, "when I tell her of your decision. I am quite certain tomorrow you will receive a letter from her asking you and your father to visit her at the Château."

He waited for Syrilla or the *Comte* to say something, but as neither of them spoke the Cardinal went on:

"I think I should explain that the *Duchesse* is in ill health—in fact it is unlikely she will live very long. I therefore suggest that the marriage is not too long delayed. Perhaps it could take place next month, in June, if it would suit you and of course—the *Duc*."

He could not help a little pause before the last words.

He would not put it past Aristide, he thought, even at the last moment to evade his responsibilities and refuse to marry the girl his mother had chosen for him.

What was more, the Cardinal was quite certain that if the *Duchesse* died there would be no question of marriage, however far advanced the arrangements had already gone.

"I am prepared to do whatever the *Duc* and his mother think best," Syrilla said.

There was still that almost unnatural radiance in her face that the Cardinal could not understand.

He could not credit for one moment that Syrilla, as the daughter of her father and mother, was interested in acquiring an important title.

Yet one never knew with women. Perhaps the zenith of her ambition was to be a *Duchesse*.

But even as he thought of it the Cardinal was sure this was not true.

No—there was something else—something he did not understand in her quick acceptance of the *Duc*'s offer and the manner in which the prospect of this marriage seemed to have made her rapturous.

'But who could feel rapture at the thought of marrying the *Duc* de Savigne?' he thought cynically.

Who but a girl quite ignorant of the social world could never have heard of the things that were said about him or the depths of degradation to which he had sunk?

As if he realised his daughter was finding it hard to speak, the *Comte* said:

"We shall wait until we hear from the *Duchesse,* and I will of course discuss this matter further with Syrilla when you have gone, to be quite certain that this is really what she wants to do."

The Cardinal felt sure that the *Comte* himself had no knowledge of the *Duc*'s reputation.

At the same time, he could not help suspecting that, because they had been so close in the past and because the *Comte* was a perceptive man, there was something not straightforward in the offer the Cardinal had made.

Perhaps he guessed that his heart was not wholly in it.

And yet the die was cast.

There was nothing the Cardinal could do now in the face of Syrilla's acceptance but to carry the news back to the Château Savigne, knowing that the *Duchesse* would rejoice in what he had to tell her.

The only trouble was that he felt a traitor—positively a Judas—to his old friend.

He told himself that he had been quite certain that if the *Comte* had not refused him Syrilla would have; and yet he had achieved what he had set out to do and wondered why his success should taste like dust and ashes.

'Perhaps she will change her mind,' he thought, to comfort himself.

Finally as he said his good-byes and the *Comte* with Syrilla standing beside him waved from the steps of the Château, the Cardinal leant forward to wave in return.

As he did so he thought that Syrilla in her white gown, her fair hair silhouetted against the grey stone of the Castle, looked almost as if she did not belong to this world.

She might have been a nymph risen from the silver water in which the Castle was reflected, or an angel who had dropped from the skies to bemuse the mere mundane humans of this world.

But Syrilla and Aristide de Savigne!

The Cardinal shuddered at the thought, and like ghouls haunting him he saw the headlines in the newspapers in which the *Duc*'s scandalous exploits were reported by pens dipped in vitriol.

He saw a procession of women with whom the *Duc*'s name had been linked, many of whom had cursed him openly and had suffered both mentally and physically because they had lost their hearts and their minds in his company.

But Syrilla, young, fresh, innocent, and as pure as the flowers, was to confront a man to whom vice was a constant companion and "love" an unknown word!

"God forgive me! I have committed a crime for which there can be no forgiveness," the Cardinal told himself.

Even his prayers were no solace as he recited them while the carriage rolled on toward Château Savigne.

Chapter Three

As Syrilla approached the bed, the *Duchesse Douairière* opened her eyes.

For a moment she looked at the vision of white beside her. Then as Syrilla raised her hand to her lips she asked:

"You are married?"

"Yes, *Belle-mère,* we are married," Syrilla replied softly.

Life seemed to come back into the *Duchesse*'s eyes and the colour to her face.

'I have been praying that you would make each other happy," she said. "Where is Aristide?"

"He will be coming to see you later, *Belle-mère,*" Syrilla answered. "Not all the guests have left."

She had refrained from distressing her mother-in-law by telling her that, when she and the *Duc* had driven back the short distance to the Château from the Chapel in the grounds, he had stepped out first and while the footmen were assisting her with her full gown and long train he had walked into the Hall and disappeared.

Syrilla could hardly believe as the guests began to arrive that he would not help her to receive them, and she told herself that it must be because he was feeling ill.

It had indeed been very hot in the Chapel, which was filled to overflowing.

The guests in their silks and satins were packed so closely and the scent of perfume mingling with the heavy fragrance of flowers and incense was overpowering.

Syrilla herself had felt as if she could hardly breathe.

The Brussels-lace veil which had been in the Monceau family for generations contributed to this, and she had hoped that when it was raised from her face she would not look too hot and flushed for the *Duc*'s first glance at her.

But when the moment came she knew that he had not looked in her direction, and driving back to the Château in the open carriage he concentrated on waving languidly to the employees and tenants on his side of the carriage.

Always perceptive where other people's feelings were concerned, Syrilla was well aware from the moment she reached his side at the steps of the Chancel that something was perturbing him.

There were vibrations emanating from him that were very different from the excitement and awe which she felt herself as she approached the Sacrament of Marriage.

She had accepted the fact that the *Duc* found it impossible to meet her before the ceremony, and the excuse that he was kept in Paris on important affairs seemed to her entirely valid.

He father indeed was perturbed and more than once the *Comte* asked her with a worried expression on his face if she was really sure she wished to be married to the *Duc*.

"I would have liked to meet him before you actually became his wife," he said quite reasonably.

"I know, Papa, but what I am sure makes it impossible for him to visit us is that the wedding, owing to his mother's health, must take place so quickly."

"You have all the rest of your lives together," the *Comte* complained. "I should have thought a few days' delay would not matter."

"The Cardinal has made all the arrangements," Syrilla replied.

She did not wish to argue with her father and when he continued to discuss the matter she was silent.

He looked at her curiously, knowing that she had changed in a way for which he could not account.

When he tried to question her about her reasons for wishing to marry the *Duc*, he found for the first time in their lives there was a barrier between them, and although he longed for her to confide in him she did not do so.

He comforted himself with the fact that when she was married she would not be far away. It took only a little over an hour to reach the Château Savigne from Monceau-sur-Indre.

Yet nothing could really console him in his knowledge that he would miss Syrilla desperately, however engrossed he might be with his books.

There was a light in Syrilla's eyes and a smile on her lips which made everybody who knew her think that they had never seen her look more lovely or appear happier.

When she received the guests in the huge Ball-room of the Château there was hardly a person who did not remark on her beauty.

As the carriages came up the long drive and turned in the courtyard to deposit their colourful occupants in front of the wide sweep of marble steps of the Château, Pierre de Bethune came to Syrilla's side.

She was standing in the place appointed, which was banked with roses and lilies, and wondering shyly what she should do as there was still no sign of the *Duc*.

"I am *Monsieur le Duc*'s Comptroller," Pierre de Bethune explained. "May I suggest, *Madame la Duchesse*, that as I cannot find the *Duc* for the moment your father should start receiving the guests at your side?"

"You do not know where *Monsieur* is?" Syrilla asked, her blue eyes worried as she raised them to Pierre de Bethune's.

"I think he must be somewhere in the grounds," he said, "and I am sure he will return before long."

"Yes, of course," Syrilla agreed, "and it would be kind of you to ask Papa to stand beside me."

Her father came at once at Pierre de Bethune's invitation, and she knew as he took his place beside her that he was extremely surprised at the bridegroom's behaviour.

There was however no chance of discussing it, because the guests, announced by a Major Domo in stentorian tones, began to pour into the Ball-Room.

There was hardly anyone whom Syrilla had met before, and she wished that she could have been greeting instead the servants, farmers, and tenants, among whom she had many acquaintances and who were being entertained in the great Tythe barn which adjoined the Home Farm.

After the Reception, three hundred people sat down to luncheon in the magnificent Banqueting Hall that had been built in mediaeval times and was one of the largest in Touraine.

There was still no sign of the *Duc,* and sitting at the top of the table with an empty chair beside her Syrilla would have felt embarrassed and a little lost if everyone had not done everything possible to make her feel at ease.

At the same time, she felt that the meal, as course succeeded course, was far too long.

The food was superlative, as might be expected.

The Chefs at the Château had been working for weeks preparing the dishes which were the specialties of the province.

There was *carpe à la Chambord,* the big, ugly carp from one of the lakes prepared according to a recipe of the Chef of François I.

Langue de boeuf en paupiette—stuffed ox-tongue rolls—was a favourite from the table of Henry II, but most of the dishes of Touraine represented the classic simplicity of country cooking.

As Syrilla expected, there was the popular black pudding of Tours, huge salmon caught in the Loire, jellied chicken livers which were very popular in Amboise, besides *Civets*—game stews and gibelotes—and rabbit fricassees beloved by those who lived in Bourgueil.

The Vouvray blanc or the Bourgueil rouge, which came from the *Duc*'s vineyard, as everybody assured Syrilla, was better than any other that was grown locally and there was no doubt that the guests were all enjoying themselves.

Only Syrilla felt that there was something very wrong in the bridegroom's absence and she could only hope that in some way she did not understand she was not the cause of his disappearance.

It was Pierre de Bethune who told her that the *Duchesse Douairière* wished to see them both as soon as it was possible for them to go to her rooms.

It had been, Syrilla knew, a bitter disappointment to the *Duchesse* that she could not actually see her son married.

"I must be well! I will be well!" she had said over and over again as soon as the date of the ceremony had been chosen.

But owing to the heat and the fact that every day she seemed to look a little more frail, the doctors had been adamant in saying that it would be too much for her.

On her various visits to the Château since her engagement had been announced, Syrilla had learnt how sensitive the *Duchesse* was about anything that concerned the *Duc*.

She would not for anything in the world have upset her mother-in-law by relating how strangely he had behaved after the wedding ceremony.

'It was kind of you to come and see me," the *Duchesse* said in her soft voice.

"I would have come long before if I could," Syrilla answered, "but I thought the meal would never end and everybody ate as if they had never seen food before!"

She gave a little laugh and her dimples showed as she added:

"I would not be in the least surprised, *Belle-mère,* if they had not been fasting for a week in anticipation of the feast they would enjoy here!

"Has the Cardinal left?" the *Duchesse* asked.

"His Eminence was obliged to return to Paris the moment the ceremony was over. I wish you could have heard his address: it was very sincere and very inspiring."

"I am sure it was."

"And so was the Service."

Syrilla felt as if the Nuptial Mass had brought a special blessing to her marriage.

Yet even when she was carried away by the beauty and the solemnity of it, she was still conscious that the man kneeling beside her was somehow unmoved by the whole Service.

She told herself she was just being imaginative, and yet she knew she was not mistaken.

"You must go back to your guests, my dearest child," the *Duchesse* said. "Thank you for coming to see me, and tell Aristide to visit me as soon as he can get away."

"Yes . . . of course . . . *Belle-mère*."

Syrilla bent and kissed her mother-in-law's cheek. Then curtseying she also kissed her hand before she turned and left the room.

As she went, the *Duchesse* was praying again that this beautiful girl would bring her son the happiness she longed for him to find.

Letting herself out of the *Duchesse*'s room, Syrilla walked along the broad corridor which led from the South Wing towards the other parts of the building.

She was sure that by now nearly all the guests would have gone and she thought that no-one would mind if she went to her own bed-room to remove the huge tiara of diamonds which she wore on her head.

It was very heavy and had obviously been intended for someone larger and stronger than herself. She would in fact have been far happier if she could have worn a conventional wreath of orange blossoms.

But the *Duchesse* had told her that it was the tiara that was always worn by the brides of the de Savignes.

Because Syrilla wished to do everything that was expected of her she would not have thought of refusing to follow the family tradition.

She had however been quite adamant that she would not wear the other overwhelming jewellery which were heirlooms: the necklace of diamonds, each one almost the size of a centime, the long ropes of perfect pearls which seemed to hold strange lights in them, the bracelets, the enormous rings!

She looked down now at the plain gold circle which the *Duc* had put on her finger and felt it was all the jewellery she wanted and she would treasure it more than anything else.

She had felt herself tremble when his hands held hers as they made their marriage vows, and behind her veil she looked at his face and thought as she had expected that he was one of the most handsome and attractive men it was possible to imagine.

The Cardinal had joined them together, saying: *"Ego conjungo vos in Matrimonium, in Nomine Patris, et Filii, et Spiritus Sancti."*

Then having blessed the pieces of gold and silver and the ring, the Cardinal had handed them to the *Duc*, who had placed the ring on Syrilla's finger, saying:

"With this ring I thee wed: this gold and silver I thee give; with my body I thee worship; and with all my wordly goods I thee endow."

Syrilla felt herself quiver as he spoke the words in a deep voice, and prayed from the very depths of her soul that she might be worthy of him and that he would love her.

Now she told herself that when all the guests had gone they would be alone and they could talk intimately with each other.

She had reached the center of the Château and from the top of the stairs she could see through the open door there were only two or three carriages left outside.

She was just about to go to her bed-room, which was known as *La Chambre de la Reine,* as it adjoined *La Chambre du Roi,* where the *Duc* slept, when she heard voices.

She was passing one of the State Rooms where the guests had left their wraps and she realised that there were two ladies inside and wondered if it would be polite for her to say good-bye to them.

She was hesitating, wondering whether to go in or not, when she heard one of them say:

"Of course the *Duc* has never been the same since that terrible tragedy. I have heard people say that it changed him completely."

"What happened?" another voice asked.

"You must know about it," the first lady replied,

"but no, you were too young at the time. It caused a sensation, I can assure you!"

"What was it?"

"The fact that the *Duc*'s *chère amie,* a woman whom many people thought he might even marry, was strangled!"

"Strangled? But by whom?"

"By a man called Astrid."

"For what reason?"

"Jealousy!"

"Who was she?"

"A ballerina by the name of Zivana Mezlanski. She was well known in Paris, and making a name for herself on the stage, when the *Duc* fell head-over-heels in love with her."

"With a ballerina? That could hardly have pleased his mother!"

"I believe Zivana Mezlanski was a very exceptional dancer and of course the *Duc* was young and impetuous, only just twenty-one."

"You say that the woman was strangled?"

"It was of course a ghastly crime and must have been very horrible for him, but they say . . ."

The speaker's voice dropped and Syrilla could not hear exactly what she said; but she caught the last words:

" .. . women mean nothing to him now!"

She had stood listening, hardly aware of what she was doing, and as she turned to go she heard the older woman add:

"He has a special Chapel or Shrine to the woman somewhere here in the Château. All her things are preserved there, even her ballet-shoes. But no-one is allowed to enter it except himself."

"Are you serious?"

"Completely serious. Everyone talked about it at first. Then, like so many other things, it was forgotten as the years passed."

"I must say," the younger woman said with a laugh, "the *Duc* looks as if he has not forgotten and is still in mourning for his lost love. I have never seen an attractive man look more lugubrious at his wedding!"

"I thought the same," the first lady agreed. "But come along, we must go. I am sure we are the last to leave."

With a start Syrilla realised that if they left the room at once they would find her outside the door.

Picking up the front of her full skirt, she hurried away down the corridor, moving so swiftly that she was sure they would not have seen her.

She entered her own bed-room and shut the door behind her.

Then she walked to the exquisitely carved dressing-table to stare in the gilt mirror which was supported by cupids, and yet she did not see her own reflection.

Now she was beginning to understand: she thought that it should have been obvious before, and that she had been very obtuse.

Why could she not have realised, she wondered, that there was something strange in that the *Duc* did not wish to see her before the actual ceremony and that all the arrangements had been made by his mother?

She would have been very unintelligent if she had had not realised in the meetings she had had with the *Duchesse* how much she longed for her son to be married.

She had shown Syrilla portraits of him at almost every age since he was born, and it was easy to understand that what the *Duchesse* yearned for more than anything else was that her only son should have children.

Again and again she told Syrilla that the Château was too big for only one child.

"I often thought that Aristide was a very lonely little boy," she said wistfully. "His father and I did our best. We had children to stay, we invited local boys to have lessons with him, but it was not the same as having brothers and sisters of his own."

"No, of course not," Syrilla had agreed.

"Perhaps it has . . . made him a little . . . reserved," the *Duchesse* said hesitatingly. "Perhaps he is not as effusive and . . . extroverted as many other Frenchmen."

Syrilla had not paid a great deal of attention at the time.

She had of course enjoyed seeing the portraits of the man who was to be her husband, and she had been deeply touched when the *Duchesse* had given her one.

But she had her own ideas of what the *Duc* would be like and what he would feel, and yet now . . .

She felt uncertain and unsure, and the rapture which the Cardinal had sensed in her and which had been with her ever since she had learnt that she was to marry the *Duc* was overshadowed.

* * *

The *Duc* walked into the Château by one of the windows opening out into the garden and saw with satisfaction that the guests had all left.

He was aware that the servants would be tidying up the Ball-Room and the Banqueting Hall and he proceeded to another wing where there was a great Library in which his father had always sat.

It was furnished not only with books but with some of the finest chests and tables in the house.

The sofas and chairs were deep and comfortable, and as the *Duc* threw himself down on one he thought with satisfaction that tomorrow he could return to Paris.

He was married and he hoped almost savagely that his mother was satisfied.

When he had left the Château, having agreed to accept the marriage she desired, he felt as he rode back to the city that he had been trapped.

He did not believe, despite her frail appearance, that his mother was as ill as she wished him to think, and when the Cardinal visited him in his Paris Mansion he suspected who it was he had to thank for the position in which he now found himself.

"Your future bride is very beautiful, my dear boy," the Cardinal told him.

The *Duc*'s lips had twisted disdainfully.

He was quite certain that his idea of a beautiful woman and the Cardinal's were very different. Besides, Paris was full of beautiful women, and nowhere were there more of them to be found than in his own house.

There was, however, only one thing about which he was curious.

"Why, Your Eminence," he asked, "did you choose a de Monceau as my future wife? I should have thought a daughter of the *Duc* de Foucauld-Fleury would have been more suitable. Their blood is already linked with ours, some centuries ago."

"The *Duc*'s only unmarried daughter is already affianced," the Cardinal replied.

"Indeed! Then let me see, who else is there in this benighted province? God knows, there are enough famous houses cheek by jowl which you could have taken your choice."

The contempt in the *Duc*'s voice stung the Cardinal into telling the truth.

"The *Viscomte* de Boulancourt's daughter's engagement was announced in the papers a week before I called on them," he replied, "and the *Marquis* d'Urville informed me categorically that he would rather see his daughter dead than let her become your wife!"

If His Eminence had hoped to shock the *Duc* he was mistaken.

The *Duc* merely flung back his head and laughed,

and it seemed for the moment that he forgot his languor and his cynical indifference.

"Good for d'Urville!" he exclaimed. "At least he is truthful. I imagine that the *Comte* de Monceau really feels the same, except that a Dukedom was too appetising a bait to be refused."

"On the contrary," the Cardinal said, "neither my friend the *Comte* de Monceau nor his daughter know anything about your reputation."

The *Duc* looked sceptical and the Cardinal said:

"That is the truth, I assure you. The *Comte* is a recluse and his daughter is completely innocent of the world outside the small village in which they live."

"How delightful!" the *Duc* had sneered. "A bovine wench who thinks only of the soil and doubtless smells like it!"

For a moment the blood rushed to the Cardinal's head and he felt a very un-Christian desire to strike the sneer from the *Duc*'s lips.

Then a wise instinct which had always stood him in good stead told him to say no more.

Let the *Duc* find out for himself what Syrilla was like. A "bovine wench" indeed! He would soon discover that he was mistaken!

The *Duc* realised, having missed his midday meal, that he was both hungry and thirsty.

He rose to tug at the bell-pull, then settled himself once again in the arm-chair.

A servant came into the room and looked surprised at seeing him.

"You rang, *Monsieur le Duc?"*

"I want something to eat and a bottle of our best wine."

The man hurried away to obey his order, and the *Duc*, looking round the room, recalled an occasion many years ago when his father had been sitting at the desk and his mother on the sofa.

He heard his own voice telling them about a girl he had met in Paris.

"She is beautiful, Mama! Exquisite! And although she is a ballerina she is in fact the daughter of a Russian nobleman."

"Then why is she on the stage?" his father asked without turning round.

"Because she has such an exceptional talent her parents allowed her to train with the Imperial Russian Ballet. As you know, dancers in Russia have a different status from what they have in this country."

"Is she very beautiful?" his mother had asked.

"I want you to see her, Mama. May I bring her home when she can get away from the theatre? They are rehearsing for a new ballet, but I might be able to persuade her to come to the country for Saturday night and perhaps Sunday."

There was only the slightest hesitation before the *Duchesse* replied:

"But of course, Aristide dearest, your friends are always welcome here."

He had a feeling at the time that there would be an argument later between his father and mother over the invitation, but as he had got what he wanted he kissed his mother and went from the Library into the garden.

Every flower, every movement of the leaves blowing in the breeze, had made him think of Zivana.

Never had he imagined that it was possible for any woman to move so exquisitely or have an allurement that seemed at times to make her enchanted.

"She has captured not only my heart but also my imagination," he told himself.

Nothing could be a better setting for her beauty than the great stone Château which had belonged to his ancestors, and the twin lakes reflecting the spires, the turrets, and the statues on its roof.

"God, but I am happy!" he exclaimed as Zivana

and his home seemed indivisibly linked in his mind, and the thought that no man had ever been more fortunate.

His memories were interrupted by the servants bringing in big trays of food, setting the dishes down on a side table. But now the *Duc* decided he was no longer hungry.

"Pour out the wine," he said, "and inform *Madame la Duchesse* that I wish to see her."

The servant bowed in acknowledgement of the command and the *Duc* drank down the glass of wine.

He was thinking as he did so that the sooner he fulfilled the duty that was required of him the quicker he could return to the life with which he was familiar and which he had deliberately chosen.

He realised that he had no idea what his bride looked like. His mother had told him when he arrived the previous evening that there was among the wedding presents a portrait of her given him by the *Comte,* but he had not been interested enough to look for it.

"What does it matter what she is like?" he asked himself. "After tonight I can leave her."

There had only been one woman who had really mattered in his life, and she . . .

His lips tightened and there was a darkness in his expression as he drank deeply from the glass he held.

The ghosts from the past etched the lines under his eyes more deeply than they had been before and the cynical disdain on his face made him appear almost sinister.

He rose and as he did so saw himself reflected in a mirror on the other side of the room.

Mockingly he raised his glass.

"Here's to posterity!" he jeered, "and a future *Duc* to carry on the name I have embellished so nobly!"

His glass was still raised when he heard the door open behind him.

For a moment he did not turn, and when he did

so he thought he must be mistaken, for this was not the wife he expected but a young girl who was little more than a child.

She stood looking at him and he stared incredulously at the fair hair that was like sunlight against the book-lined walls, the blue eyes, and the translucent purity of her skin.

For a moment they held each other's eyes. Then impulsively, as if she was eager to reach his side, Syrilla moved towards him.

The *Duc* was to much a connoisseur of women not to notice the grace of her slender body and the manner in which her small head was poised on a long neck.

She swept to the ground in a deep curtsey, and as she rose she said:

"*Monseigneur!* I have wanted so much to talk to you!"

The *Duc* stared at her.

"What—did you call me?"

A faint flush rose in Syrilla's cheeks as she answered:

"*Monseig . . . neur.*"

"That is the title usually reserved for dignitaries of the Church or Princes of the Royal blood."

"I am aware of that . . . but it is the . . . way I have . . . always thought of you."

"Always?" he questioned.

"Ever since I first saw you."

The *Duc* raised his eye-brows.

"I do not recall any meeting."

Syrilla laughed.

"You were hardly likely to. I said that I saw you and that is the truth, but you were not likely to notice me amongst a crowd of a thousand—no, perhaps two thousand other people."

The *Duc* gestured with a hand towards the sofa.

"Suppose you sit down and tell me about it?" he suggested.

Syrilla did as he asked and the *Duc* leant back in the arm-chair he had recently vacated.

His eyes were on Syrilla's face.

'The Cardinal was right,' he thought, 'she is certainly unusually beautiful, but God knows what I have in common with a child of that age.'

Not that it was of any importance, since he was returning to Paris tomorrow.

"What were you going to tell me?" he prompted as Syrilla was silent.

"I was just thinking that you look exactly as you did nine years ago . . . no . . . that is not true. You look sad, which you did not then . . . and that I . . . understand."

"I do not follow you," the *Duc* said. "Tell me where you first saw me."

"I should have thought you might have guessed," Syrilla said. "At the Tournament that was given here in the Château grounds on your twenty-first birthday!"

"But of course," he exclaimed, "I had forgotten about it. My father and mother revived the jousts that had taken place in mediaeval times."

"And you were the Knight . . . the White Knight," Syrilla said softly.

There was an expression in her eyes which told the *Duc,* as did the note in her voice, that she had been moved by his appearance in the shining armour that had belonged to one of his ancestors.

The jousting had been skilfully arranged and meticulously rehearsed.

The Black Knight, his opponent, had gained two minor victories, then he had challenged him, and of course, because it was all play-acting, won when good triumphed over evil.

He could remember now the cheers and applause that had gone up from the stands and the crowd that had come from far and near throughout Touraine to be present at such an auspicious occasion.

The crowd had been jolly, noisy, and good-humoured, filled with beer and cider which his father dispensed liberally, while in the stands all the beautiful young women from the adjacent Castles had been attired in mediaeval costume.

The *Duc* recalled carrying the favour of some lady who presented it to him formally, but he had thought romantically as he fought that the favour which mattered was Zivana's miniature, which he carried in a locket round his neck.

Perhaps because he was fighting for someone he loved, it had made him appear very dashing and certainly as romantic as everyone wished him to be.

"Nine years ago," he said to himself reflectively.

"I was nine, too," Syrilla said, "and I have never forgotten how you looked . . . and you . . . inspired everyone who saw you."

"It was only a performance."

There was silence for a moment. Then Syrilla said:

"May I tell you . . . something, *Monseigneur,* now that we are . . . alone?"

"Yes, of course," the *Duc* replied. "There has not been a chance of our having any conversation until now."

"I did not understand . . . I did not know until a little while ago . . . what you felt."

The *Duc* looked puzzled.

He could hardly imagine that his mother had told this child what his intentions were towards his wife and their future together.

He had, however, made them quite clear to his mother last night after his arrival when she had talked as if he intended to stay at the Château some length of time.

"I have obeyed your wishes, Mama," he had said in a hard voice. I am giving up my freedom because you have asked it of me, and I will endeavour to see that you have the grandchild you yearn for so ardently, but that is all!"

He paused to add firmly:

"We made a bargain, you and I, and I will fulfill my part of it."

"What do you mean, Aristide?" the *Duchesse* had asked.

"I mean that I intend to go back to Paris and to live there."

"For . . . ever?" the *Duchesse* faltered.

"For as long as it suits me," the *Duc* replied. "My wife can stay here and you can keep her company, but I do not intend that she shall in any way interfere with me any more than I shall interfere with her."

"But . . . Aristide!" the *Duchesse* cried.

"There is no point in discussing it, Mama," the *Duc* interrupted. "Nothing you can say, nothing you can do, will make me change my mind. One night should be enough to make sure that your fondest hopes are realised, and then you will have no further hold over me."

He knew as he spoke that he was being brutal. At the same time he, was fighting to free himself from the silken chains by which the *Duchesse* had endeavoured to hold him once before and failed.

There was a long silence and the *Duc* knew that his mother was fighting against the tears which threatened to overwhelm her.

He walked towards the door.

"Good-night, Mama," he had said, and left before she could say any more.

Now, he told himself, he would have to make his position clear to his wife, and he wondered how and with what words he should begin.

Because he found it difficult he said almost sharply:

"Tell me what you wish to say."

Syrilla's eyes were very large in her pointed face.

Then unexpectedly she moved from the sofa to kneel down at the *Duc*'s side.

"I did not realise," she said in a soft voice, "until now what you suffered ten years ago."

The *Duc* stiffened.

"Who told you?"

"I overheard two ladies talking after I left your mother's room," she replied. "The elder one was saying how deeply you had . . . loved, and how . . . tragically you had lost that love. Oh, *Monseigneur* . . . I now understand!"

"What do you understand?"

"That you have only married because it would please your mother, that you had dedicated yourself to an ideal, and only for your mother's sake have you fulfilled her wishes."

The *Duc* did not speak and after a moment Syrilla went on:

"I have always known that everything you did and thought would be noble, and this great love is what I might have expected of you."

The *Duc* was staring at her incredulously, but with her eyes looking up into his she continued:

"It is the pure, selfless love of the Troubadours, who dedicated themselves, as you have done, to serve the lady they worshipped until they died."

Syrilla made a little gesture with her hands.

"Now I have learnt what happened," she said in a soft voice, "I promise that I will not be any trouble, that I will help you so that no-one will ever know."

"Know what?"

"Just as your love is too sacred to be talked about by outsiders," she answered, "so the arrangement between us will also be a secret. Although I am your wife in . . . name, I will respect the . . . path you have chosen and I shall intrude as . . . little as possible."

Perhaps for the first time in his life, the *Duc* found

himself bewildered to the point when he could find no words in which to express himself.

The admiration which was almost adulation in Syrilla's eyes did not escape him, nor did the awed note in her voice which made it seem as if she spoke of something very sacred.

How, he asked himself, could he explain to this child that he was not dedicated to any great ideal, and that what had happened in the past had in fact turned him into the cynic he now was?

With an effort he found his voice and asked:

"Are you telling me that you think I should not actually make you my wife?"

"I know you might do so out of duty to your mother," Syrilla replied, "but I know too it would go against your deepest . . . instinct and you would feel even if you . . . kissed me that you . . . betrayed the love that is in your heart."

She looked away from him a little shyly as she said:

"The lady I was listening to said that you had a special Shrine or Chapel in this house where you had locked away all the things that belonged to the woman you loved. I can understand that your heart is in there also."

She paused for a moment before she said:

"The lady also said that women mean nothing to you now. So as I am a woman, even though legally I am your wife, I can mean nothing, and that I . . . accept."

She looked at him again as she added:

"I do not believe that any other man could be so wonderful or so noble, and having loved you ever since I was a little girl, I love and revere you now more than I can possibly express in words."

The *Duc* felt almost as if he was in a dream.

How, he asked himself, could he possibly explain that she had misinterpreted what she had overheard?

Women meant nothing to him!

He almost laughed thinking of the hundreds of women who had passed through his hands—so many in fact that in many cases he could not remember either their faces or their names.

But how could he say so to his wife, kneeling at his feet, looking up at him with an adoration she would give to a Saint.

Never, he thought, with all the women he had known, had there been one who looked at him in just that sort of way, and while it was a new experience, at the same time it made him feel uncomfortable.

With difficulty he tried to find words to explain to Syrilla that she had been mistaken.

"You saw me as the White Knight when you were the age of nine, and I was twenty-one," he said. "I am now thirty and I have changed and altered considerably in the past years."

A smile illuminated Syrilla's face.

"Of course," she answered. "Papa says that anyone who does not grow wiser every year, every month, every minute, is a fool! We are sent into the world to learn and of course as we develop we know more and I think we should feel more."

She made a little gesture as if she was afraid the *Duc* would misunderstand her.

"I can guess what you must have felt when you suffered such a tragedy. It must have torn you in pieces, but I think now you will be even more resolved in your dedication than you were then."

Her voice softened as she went on:

"And yet you were prepared to sacrifice everything you hold dear for the sake of your mother. That was very, very wonderful of you, but it is what I would have expected."

The *Duc* felt he was becoming mesmerised by what she was saying.

"I must explain, Syrilla," he said hastily, "and you

must not have such romantic notions about me. I am, after all, human and certainly not like the Knightly figure that I may have seemed in armour."

Syrilla rose to her feet and suddenly the *Duc* saw the dimples on either side of her mouth.

"Now you are going to disparage yourself and decry your own greatness, *Monseigneur*," she said, "but I am not going to listen, and please, although I know you are thinking of me . . . you are not to do so. I am content, utterly and completely content to be your wife, and to admire you because you are everything a man should be."

She did not wait for his answer but moved away across the Library to stand for the moment in one of the windows.

The sunlight illuminated her hair and the *Duc* thought for a moment she had a halo round her head, before she said with a lilt in her voice:

"There are so many things we can do together here. I want to visit your vineyards; I want you to tell me about the treasures there are in this house, for I am sure everyone of them has a history; and I want very much to see you catch a fish in the lake."

Again the dimples were in her cheeks as she said:

"You do not know what a temptation those lakes are to your neighbours. Quite a number of the gentlemen were telling me today that they are often tempted, because you are so seldom here, to poach the fat trout which lie among the reeds."

She laughed as she added:

"And one of your neighbours has actually threatened that if you do not do something about the deer, which are far too numerous, he will hunt them himself!"

'I must explain that I am leaving for Paris tomorrow morning,' the *Duc* thought, but somehow the words would not come to his lips.

He rose to his feet and as he did so Syrilla moved across the room towards him.

She slipped her hand into his with the confiding gesture of a child.

"Do you think there will be time before dinner for us to go and explore the garden?" she asked. "I have wanted to do that so much every time I have come here, but then I thought it would be more fun for us to go together."

She paused.

"I long to see where you played when you were a little boy and most of all I want to see where I first saw you, on the ground that was used for the jousting."

The *Duc* told himself it was only right that he should make an effort to please her after the way he had behaved during the wedding.

"I am sure we have time," he said, "and after all, dinner can wait until we are ready for it."

Syrilla's eyes twinkled at him.

"What will the Chefs say if we spoil their soufflés?"

"Let them spoil!" the *Duc* replied.

Chapter Four

With a little difficulty Syrilla drew her horse to a standstill and looked back to cry over her shoulder:

"I won! I won, *Monseigneur!*"

The *Duc* drew even with her, thinking he had never seen a woman who sat a horse better or despite her fragile appearance had such good hands.

They had raced in the Park over the ground where the joust had taken place and where Syrilla had seen him as the Knight in shining armour.

He had known, as soon as he saw her mounted on one of his finely bred animals with an Arabian strain in them that she was an exceptional horsewoman.

At the same time, with the stallion he was riding he could have beaten her in the race with comparative ease.

On an impulse which he did not understand himself the *Duc* had allowed Syrilla to reach the chosen goal first.

It was something he had never thought of doing in past years, having always in every way, even down to the smallest detail, wished to dominate whatever woman he was with.

"You rode well," he said as he drew his horse up alongside her's.

She looked up at him and said:

"I have a fancy, *Monseigneur,* that once again you have been chivalrous."

"You are too perceptive, or perhaps should I say too intelligent, Syrilla."

"I am sure you would not wish your wife to be anything else," she replied. "You are so clever yourself that I am afraid of boring you with my stupidity."

"How do you know I am clever?" he asked, feeling curious to hear her answer.

"Your mother has shown me all the prizes you took at school and at University."

"Book-learning, repeated parrot-wise!" the *Duc* said disparagingly.

"You do not expect me to believe that," Syrilla answered. "Papa always says that it is not what one reads which matters, but the way in which new horizons are opened up to the mind."

"I have long ago given up looking for horizons."

"That is not true," Syrilla interrupted, "and if you think me intelligent it is because I believed deep in my subconscious mind that I should one day be able to talk to you just as we are doing now."

It was extraordinary, the *Duc* was to think later in the day, that he could in fact talk with Syrilla as he had never talked with another woman.

With other women the conversation, if there had been any, had always centred round the woman herself and her attraction for him.

Every word had a double meaning, every phrase was an enticement not of the mind but of the body.

With Syrilla it was very different.

She asked him innumerable questions because she was interested and curious, but she also contributed what she herself thought and felt and the *Duc* found himself stimulated in a way in which he had not been stimulated for a long time.

He sensed that a lot of what Syrilla said derived from what she had learnt from her father.

At the same time, there were always her own original ideas and the way in which she appeared to look at things from quite a different angle from what he might have expected.

"How can you know so much about the Orient," he asked during one argument, "when from what you have told me you have never travelled?"

Syrilla's eyes twinkled at him.

"People can go round and round the world and see nothing but their own back-yards," she answered. "I would love to see the places we have been talking about. At the same time, because I have studied them I almost feel as if I have been there, they are so real to me."

"Most girls of your age would be thinking about men, not books and ruins of the past."

"I was always in fact thinking of one man," she answered, "and striving to make myself worthy of him."

The *Duc*'s expression was sceptical.

"There must have been other men in your life besides a mythical Knight whom you might never meet."

"Of course there were men," Syrilla answered. "There was the Curé who, when I wore a new bonnet in Church, always averted his eyes. I think he thought I was one of the temptations of St. Anthony!"

There were dimples on both sides of her mouth as she went on:

"Then there was Farmer Bastie's son. He once brought me half a pig to show his affection, but he blushed so red when he gave it to me that it was difficult to know which was the pig and which was the man!"

The *Duc* laughed as if he could not help it.

"You know perfectly well, Syrilla, that I am talking about *Beaux*. In the great Château near your home there must be innumerable and ardent young noblemen whom I am quite certain scoured the country in the hope of finding someone who looked like you!"

"In Monceau-sur-Indre I must have been invisible," Syrilla answered, "and I was very happy to be with Papa and think of you."

"Quite frankly, I do not believe in this obsession you had for a man you had seen only once," the *Duc* said mockingly. "You are straining my credulity, Syrilla, even though it is extremely flattering to think that one look at me when you were hardly out of the Nursery has meant to you so much all these years."

"It is true, *Monseigneur*," Syrilla said with a note of sincerity in her voice which could not have been assumed. "And remember that, although I only saw you one day, when Mama and I came to the Château there were pictures of you in many of the books in Papa's Library."

He raised his eye-brows and she explained:

"They may have been entitled 'St. George,' 'Sir Galahad,' 'Jason Searching for the Golden Fleece,' or 'Odysseus,' who had himself lashed to the mast when passing the island of the Sirens. But whoever the pictures depicted, to me they were always you."

Her eyes lit up as she went on:

"I used to tell myself stories in which you killed the dragon and did innumerable deeds of heroism and valour."

The *Duc* did not speak and after a moment she said:

"But now I think I should have imagined you as a Troubadour singing:

"If Heaven be gained by love and prayer,
Then I at once should enter there."

The *Duc* made a little sound which might have been one of exasperation, and Syrilla said quickly:

"Forgive me. Perhaps you think it is an impertinence

of me to speak of your true love. I will not do it again."

The *Duc* rose from the chair in which he had been sitting beside Syrilla after they had finished dinner to walk across the room to look at the last dying rays of the sun sinking behind the high trees.

"Nothing we could say to each other should be an impertinence, Syrilla," he said after a moment, "and I think it is important that we speak frankly, and that is why I want . . ."

He paused because he was searching for words to express what he was trying to say, but before he could find them Syrilla had sprung from the sofa to move across the room to stand beside him.

"That is what I hoped you would say, *Monseigneur.* I have always talked openly to Papa, saying anything that came into my mind, and I would hate that there should be any barriers between us. I love you, and there is nothing I can give you but my thoughts."

The *Duc* wanted to say that she could give him a great deal more; but looking into the innocence of her blue eyes he found it impossible.

Almost abruptly he changed the conversation.

"Tell me why you walk so gracefully," he said. "You must have had a lot of lessons in deportment and dancing."

Syrilla laughed .

"The only teachers of those sort of accomplishments in Monceau-sur-Indre are the birds, or perhaps the fawns in the wood."

"Are you telling me that you have not been taught to dance?" the *Duc* enquired.

To his surprise there came an anxious expression to Syrilla's face as she replied:

"I was so hoping you would not ask me that."

"Why?"

"Because, *Monseigneur,* I have never danced . . . with a man, I mean."

"You have never been to a Ball?" the *Duc* asked increduously.

"After Mama died there was no-one to take me, even if I had been asked to one," Syrilla explained. "And Papa would have hated having to put on his 'best bib and tucker' and sit on a dais with the Dowagers."

She smiled and then again there was an anxious expression on her face as she said:

"I would not wish you to be . . . ashamed of my ignorance. Perhaps we could find a teacher, so that when I am really proficient I could attend a Ball with you."

"There is no hurry for that," the *Duc* said automatically.

"I know you do not have time for such frivolities," Syrilla said, "and I was going to ask you, *Monseigneur,* whether I could possibly help you in any way with your work in Paris."

"My work?" the *Duc* questioned in surprise.

"Yes, *Belle-mère* told me about it."

"Indeed! And what did she say?"

"I asked her what you did and she said, 'My son is concerned with the people of Paris who are unfortunate.' "

The *Duc* smiled at his mother's evasion of the truth. And yet she had managed to provide her daughter-in-law with an answer to an awkward question.

"I have heard so much about the poverty and misery," Syrilla went on, "which exists in the slums and how the people are often starving, besides being wounded, perhaps killed, by the rioting."

"I believe that is true," the *Duc* said.

He was thinking that he had never concerned himself with such matters except to hope that his own property should not be damaged by the Revolutionaries.

"That is just what I would expect you to do, to help such people," Syrilla said. "Perhaps, if it was no trouble, I could come with you to Paris sometimes and see your work for myself."

The *Duc* had a sudden vision of her at one of his outrageous parties. He knew only too clearly how women like Susanne, Aimie, and Rosette would shock and at the same time bewilder her.

"I have no wish for you to come to Paris," he said sharply.

"I would not desire to do anything you would not want me to do," Syrilla replied. "At the same time, *Monseigneur,* even the most holy of men have not scorned the help of their disciples."

She smiled a little tremulously as she added:

"I am a very willing disciple . . . as you well know."

"We were speaking about dancing," the *Duc* said, "not the sordid conditions of Paris. If you do not learn to dance and never go to any of the parties to which you will undoubtedly be invited in your position as my wife, what will be the use of all those extremely pretty gowns that you have in your trousseau?"

Syrilla looked down at her gown, which was made of pink gauze with the full skirts draped and ornamented with rose-buds and pale blue ribbons.

"I have never owned such beautiful dresses before," she said. "Did you know that your mother gave them to me as a present?"

"I had no idea," the *Duc* replied.

"*Belle-mère* was so kind. She realised that living so quietly with Papa I hardly knew what the fashions were; so she sent my measurements to Paris, described what I looked like, and all these elegant and exciting gowns arrived. I was so touched by her generosity."

The *Duc* guessed that his mother's generosity lay in the fact that she wished Syrilla to attract him. There was no doubt that the gowns, which showed the whiteness of her shoulders and accentuated the tininess of her waist, made her look very lovely.

But there was something more than mere beauty

about her, he thought, which made her different from other women.

It was the fact that she was so intensely alive, and that when she was animated she seemed almost to sparkle as she spoke, while her eyes shone as if they had captured the sunlight.

"I must tell *Belle-mère* that you have admired my gowns," Syrilla said. "And . . . *Monseigneur* . . . will you forgive me if I say something very . . . personal?"

"I thought we had already agreed to be frank with each other," the *Duc* replied.

"Then will you tell your mother how much you . . . love her and how much she means to you?" Syrilla asked. "You are her whole life. She thinks and dreams and prays for you, and I think that every word you have ever said to her is carved on her heart."

The *Duc* did not reply, and after a moment Syrilla said:

"She is so happy that you are married. I think if you had refused to do as she asked, she would have died feeling she had nothing left to live for."

"Did she tell you that?" the *Duc* asked sharply.

"No, of course not," Syrilla answered, "but I knew it instinctively when she talked to me about you, and when I saw the happiness in her eyes when I went to her room in my wedding gown."

"I should have gone there with you," the *Duc* said unexpectedly.

"I understand now why you disappeared," Syrilla replied, "but you must never let your mother suspect for one moment that we are not behaving like . . . like an . . . ordinary bride and bridegroom."

"You know she wants me to have an heir?" the *Duc* asked slowly.

Syrilla nodded and he continued:

"Is it right for us to deny her something that she desires so fervently?"

He waited for Syrilla's answer, feeling surprisingly tense.

"I have . . . thought about that," she said, "and I do realise that it is important for you one day to have an . . . heir to inherit your . . . title and your vast possessions."

"And what is your solution?" the *Duc* asked.

"I thought . . . and please do not think it presumptuous of me . . . perhaps one day, when we have known each other longer, you might look upon me as a friend . . . and feel that as a friend I could . . . give you a child."

The words were spoken very softly, then before the *Duc* could reply Syrilla went on:

"I know it will be difficult for you to think of me in such a way, and I am not quite . . . certain how a man and a woman . . . make love so that they have . . . a baby."

There was a little pause before she continued:

"But although you cannot ever . . . love me or give me your heart . . . it would be wonderful . . . very . . . very wonderful for me to have your . . . child."

The *Duc* took a step forward. Then before he could touch Syrilla she said:

"I am only speaking of something that may happen in the . . . future. It may be years before you feel you can . . . touch me in such a way . . . and I would not like you to think that I am not conscious of your goodness or the sacred dedication of your vow of chastity."

She did not understand the expression on the *Duc*'s face and she said quickly:

"P-please forgive me that I . . . spoke of this again, but you did . . . ask me and once again I am telling you of my thoughts."

"And I am listening to you with great interest, Syrilla."

This was the opportunity, the *Duc* told himself, when he should make things very clear to her.

But somehow like quicksilver the moment evaded him and he found himself talking of other matters and unable to direct the conversation back again to the channels he wanted.

Later, however, when he went to his own room, he was determined that there should be no more shilly-shallying.

He would make it clear to Syrilla once and for all that he was her husband and intended to behave as such.

He thought how much he would laugh at another man if he was told how the poetic dreams of a young girl prevented him from making love to her and treating her as a man should treat the woman who was his wife.

A number of bawdy anecdotes concerning impotent husbands came to his mind, and he decided that he would have no more nonsense, and what was more, the sooner he returned to Paris the better!

As his valets helped him undress, his own thoughts mocked and jeered at him. He told himself he must be growing senile if after being the lover of every woman who took his fancy he could not explain to a girl of eighteen what he wanted of her.

'It is simply because she is unsophisticated that I find it so difficult,' he thought, 'but doubtless she is like every other woman, acting a part, and by no means as innocent as she appears.'

Yet while he scoffed at his own hesitation he knew that no woman, however brilliant an actress, could produce the expression of adoration in her eyes which Syrilla had when she looked at him, or force such a note of sincerity into her voice.

"The whole concept of me as a Knight in shining armour is absurd!" the *Duc* asserted when his valets left him alone. "God knows, if any of my friends heard Syrilla talking in such a manner, they would laugh their heads off!"

He knew his reputation better than his critics did. He was well aware of the results of every outrageous exploit and he read the newspaper reports of his behaviour with amusement.

He had deliberately set out to defy the conventions, to shock decent men and women, to become a by-word for everything that was debauched and immoral.

He had succeeded, but strangely enough it had not eased the hurt which had caused him to behave in such a manner, and the wound within himself had not healed.

"Curse it, but I am getting morbid!" the *Duc* said aloud.

He looked round the great room with its carved panels, its painted ceiling, and the huge canopied velvet bed with the Royal Coat-of-Arms embellished above the headboard.

Suddenly he felt furiously angry.

"It is this damned house!" he cursed. "It is the ghosts of my ancestors peering over my shoulder! I will go back to the sewers of Paris, where I belong and where I feel most at home."

It was as if he defied and challenged his forefathers.

Yet he felt as if they were reaching out to him from the grave, striving to draw him back into their circle and under their influence.

They were calling to him. He could almost hear their voices and see the pity and condemnation in their eyes.

"I will not listen to you!" he wanted to shout. "I have escaped you once and I will escape again!"

He picked up a candle from the bed-side and the movement made the flame flicker and the grease ran down over the gold candlestick and from there to the carpet.

Turning, the *Duc* pulled open the communicating

door which connected *la Chambre du Roi* to *la Chambre de la Reine.*

Between the two rooms there was a narrow passage in which there were wardrobes, a powder-closet, and a bath-room for the use of the *Duc*. The one attached to *la Chambre de la Reine* was on the other side of the Suite.

He moved along the passage, his feet making no sound on the thick carpet.

He was wearing a velvet robe over his night-shirt and his feet were encased in velvet slippers embroidered with his Insignia.

It was many years since he had opened the door into *la Chambre de la Reine,* in fact not since he had been a child and his mother and father had used these rooms.

In the morning he would run happily up and down the passage between them, first to nibble at his mother's breakfast, then to watch his father being shaved by his valet.

His mother's room had always smelt fragrant from the flowers which stood in big bowls on the gilded tables whatever the time of year, and the perfume she had used had a very distinctive scent all of its own.

It seemed to the *Duc* that he smelt now the fragrance of flowers, but the perfume was different.

It was one that he had noticed on Syrilla earlier in the evening, and it reminded him of spring flowers. He thought in fact that it was jasmine, one of the first heralds of the spring.

He realised that he had been sitting in his own room for so long that it must be quite late.

As his hand went out towards Syrilla's door he suspected that she might be asleep and he did not wish to frighten her.

He turned the handle very gently and as the door opened he looked into the room.

But Syrilla was not asleep, and one glance at the

huge bed draped in silk, the pale azure blue of Sèvres china, showed that it was empty.

Then by the light of the candles burning on either side he saw that Syrilla was kneeling on the *Prie-Dieu,* the Prayer Stool, which stood facing the wall opposite the bed.

It had been there in his mother's time, but he had actually never seen her praying on it.

Syrilla was kneeling there now, wearing only her white nightgown, the lights of the candles picking out the gold in her hair.

The fingers of her hands were pressed together like a child's and although she was kneeling upright her head was bowed and her eyes were closed.

The *Duc* stood looking at her, then suddenly she raised her head and looked at the picture above the *Prie-Dieu.*

The *Duc* knew it well.

It was a copy which one of his ancestors had brought home from Florence of a picture by Botticelli and was called *The Magnificat.*

It had been his favourite picture as a child. The Madonna held the baby on her lap, surrounded by angels who held a crown over her head.

It was then that the *Duc* realised that Syrilla's beauty had the same spirituality that could be seen in the faces of the angels painted by Botticelli.

Quite unaware that he was watching her, she had a radiance in her face that was not of this world.

He knew without being told for whom she prayed and what she asked for in her prayers.

Then as if her purity erected an invisible barrier between them which he dared not pass, he shut the door quietly and went back to his own bed-room.

* * *

The *Duc* was breakfasting in the sunshine in a small

oval-shaped room that was kept exclusively for the first meal of the day.

He had just helped himself liberally to a dish of *Fritures*—small fried fish from the Loire—when Syrilla came into the room.

"Please . . . do not move, *Monseigneur*," she begged as the Duc began to rise from his chair. "I am early, but it is such a lovely day and I am longing to ride with you as you promised we should do . . . to the vineyards."

"I had not forgotten," the *Duc* replied. "In fact I sent a message an hour ago to tell my manager to expect us. I am sure he will want us to sample all the different vintages we have in the wine-caves, so you must be careful not to fall off your horse on the way home!"

"I do not think I should drink very much," Syrilla said seriously.

"I will prevent you from doing that," the *Duc* replied.

She smiled at him in a way which made him think any man would be only too anxious to take care of her.

"You have had breakfast?" he asked.

"Yes, thank you," she replied, "but not such a substantial meal as yours. Dare I steal one of your *croissants?* And I never thought of asking for honey. I am sure the honey from your bees is better than from anyone else's in the whole of Touraine."

She did not wait for his permission and spread a *croissant* with butter and honey.

"If I listened to you, I should become very conceited, not only about myself but also about my possessions," the *Duc* said in an amused voice.

"And why not?" she asked. "They are better than anyone else's! Why only yesterday I heard your Headgroom saying there was not a horse between here and Nice to equal the one you were riding."

The *Duc* laughed.

"And doubtless my herdsman thinks that my cows give better milk and my cattle better beef than any other animal between here and Cherbourg!"

"I am sure they are right," Syrilla said quite seriously. "And the guests at the wedding kept exclaiming how delicious your wines were!"

The *Duc* finished what he was eating and said:

"I cannot remember having such a large appetite for years. I suspect the air here also is better than anywhere else!"

He was teasing Syrilla.

At the same time, he knew quite well it was not the inferior air of Paris that prevented him from having an appetite in the morning, but the amount he drank the night before and the excesses in which he indulged.

Now he felt unexpectedly athletic and healthy as he followed Syrilla across the Hall, where he was handed his hat, his riding-whip, and his gloves.

Their horses were waiting outside, and he thought that Syrilla's riding-habit of white piqué, which was the latest fashion in Paris, was even more becoming to her than the pale green one which she had worn the day before.

The groom helped her into the saddle and the *Duc* was just about to mount his stallion, which was resisting the efforts of two grooms to hold him steady and bucking in the most obstreperous manner, when Pierre de Bethune came running down the steps.

"There is a letter from Paris, *Monsieur,* which needs your immediate attention," he said to the *Duc*.

"Immediate?" the *Duc* questioned.

"It is said to be of the utmost urgency, and the groom is waiting to carry your reply back to *Monsieur* Layfette."

This was the name of the *Duc*'s Lawyer, and if Pierre said the matter was one of urgency, then it must be.

He looked at Syrilla, whose horse was already fidgeting to be off, and said:

"Ride on slowly. I will catch you up."

She smiled at him and cried:

"Please do not keep *Monseigneur* long, *Monsieur* de Bethune. We have so much to see before luncheon."

"I will be as quick as I can, *Madame,*" Pierre promised.

There was a look of admiration in his eyes that was unmistakable as he spoke. Then he hurried after the *Duc,* who was already striding impatiently back up the steps into the house.

"What is it?" he asked as Pierre joined him, and they walked side by side towards his office, which was a short way down one of the corridors.

"It is trouble, I am afraid, *Monsieur.*"

"What sort of trouble?" the *Duc* asked curtly.

Pierre de Bethune handed him a letter which had come from his Lawyer and he read it with a frown on his face.

A woman, one of the more disreputable of the *Cocottes* whom he had entertained and for a very short while had captured his fancy, had been arrested.

The Police had found in her possession a number of articles that she had taken from the different men with whom she had slept, some of which were very valuable.

From the *Duc* she had stolen an emerald ring bearing his monogram, several gold ornaments equally easily identifiable, and some sapphire and diamond cuff-links.

What the Lawyer had said in his letter to the *Duc* was that the Police wished him and every other man from whom the woman had stolen to support a charge against her.

This would mean her getting a long term of imprisonment, but it would also result in their names being mentioned in Court.

The *Duc* read the letter through slowly. Then he said:

"I do not mind losing the jewellery, but the gold ornaments are part of the family collection. They were in fact given to one of my ancestors by Charlemagne. I dislike the thought of losing them."

"Do you not think it possible, *Monsieur,* for the Police to return them to you without your bringing a case against the woman?"

"She will tell the Police that I gave them to her. Those women always make some excuse," the *Duc* answered.

"Then you will prosecute?"

The *Duc* hesitated.

He did not know why, but he had a sudden dislike of letting all Paris know that he had been associated with a woman who was not only a *Cocotte* but also a petty thief.

She had her attractions, he was not denying that, but at the same time it seemed to him particularly sordid that while he had been asleep she had taken the cuff-links from his discarded shirt.

He thought for a moment. Then he said sharply:

"I will not prosecute. Notify all jewellers and those to whom such creatures sell their stolen goods that I am prepared to buy back any pieces which carry the Savigne Coat-of-Arms."

"I hoped you would say that, *Monsieur*."

The *Duc* raised his eye-brows.

"Why, Pierre?"

Just for a moment he thought his Comptroller would not tell him the truth, but then almost defiantly Pierre de Bethune said:

"*Madame la Duchesse* might hear of it, and it would —hurt her."

There was silence and Pierre wondered if the *Duc* would annihilate him for speaking the truth as he had done so often before.

But to his surprise the *Duc* merely said quietly:

"Yes, Pierre, it would hurt her."

He turned to hurry after Syrilla, but outside the Comptroller's office he found his Agent waiting for him.

The man had a list of complaints from tenants who considered their rents were too high in relation to the repairs their landlord did for them.

It took the *Duc* some time to extricate himself, and when finally he mounted the stallion, who was now behaving even more skittishly, Syrilla was out of sight.

* * *

Syrilla had not meant to go so far from the Château, but the horse she was riding was fresh and wished to gallop.

When she looked back she realised she could no longer see the great house.

She had ridden to the edge of the Park and in front of her there were now thick woods. She thought that the cutting through them which she and the *Duc* would take to the vineyards lay to the left.

However, she had no intention of going any further without the *Duc* and she turned back to look for him. But as she did so, from the shelter of the trees a number of men appeared.

She looked at them in surprise, seeing that they were ordinary labourers, but all of them carried long sticks in their hands and one or two even held ancient pikes.

To her astonishment, they surrounded her horse and one man put his hand on the bridle.

"Who are you . . . what do you want?" Syrilla asked.

"Where's the *Duc?*" a man asked.

He was an uncouth-looking individual with long

hair hanging almost to his shoulders and wearing clothes which were tattered and torn.

The other men were of similar appearance and the expressions on their faces as they looked at her made Syrilla feel uneasy.

There had been no sign in Monceau-sur-Indre two years ago of the Revolution, but that had not prevented Syrilla from reading descriptions of what had taken place in other parts of the country.

She knew that in Paris two thousand soldiers and people had been killed and over five thousand wounded.

There had been casualties in every town in France and desperate fighting, as she had learnt from her mother's relations in Calvados in Normandy.

The man who had his hand on her bridle started to pull the horse forward into the wood.

"What are you doing?" Syrilla demanded.

"Ye're comin' wi' us," the man answered.

"You cannot take me away!" Syrilla cried. "This, as you must well know, will do you no good. If you have something to say to the *Duc,* come to the Château and ask him to listen to you."

"And get whipped or shot down for our pains?" the man asked jeeringly. "We meant to take the *Duc* this mornin', but like enough ye'll do as well. After all, 'tis only right that the new *Duchesse* should see how her people live."

He spoke in a way that was singularly unpleasant and Syrilla thought it would be a mistake to bandy words with him.

The other men were muttering amongst themselves, and they all looked so rough and unpleasant that she knew there was nothing she could do but let them take her where they wished.

Even if the *Duc* should find her now, she was afraid for him: the stout sticks and the pikes which the men carried would prove effective weapons against a man who carried nothing but a riding-whip.

Quite suddenly the crimes perpetrated by the Revolutionaries swept into her mind to start her heart beating faster.

It was not only the heads that had tumbled in the baskets under the guillotine thirty-nine years ago. There had also been innumerable instances since of aristocrats who lived in the country being beaten up and even killed by the peasants, and in some cases their wives and children had been shown no mercy.

Although her lips were dry, she held her chin high and tried not to hear the rude comments of some of the men and the coarse jokes they made to each other as they walked along behind her.

They emerged on the other side of the wood and now Syrilla had a view of the *Duc*'s vineyards stretching away for what appeared to be miles.

The vines were in leaf and the bunches of grapes, although still small and green, were easily discernible, giving evidence that there would be a good vintage that year.

On reaching the vineyards the men surrounding her turned right and moved away from the broad acres down the side of the wood. After some time they came to a valley that was hidden by trees and which had a small, insignificant stream running through it.

They had been moving at a quick rate for over half an hour when Syrilla saw ahead what appeared to be a small village.

There were vines growing round it, and then as they grew nearer she saw that the vines were different in appearance from those they had passed earlier on.

There were no leaves on the brown roots, no buds, no young shoots.

"Are you lookin' round you?" the man who was walking beside her asked savagely. "You come from this part o' the world, I believes, and you knows what a vine should look like when you sees one."

"I can see these are dead . . . or dying," Syrilla answered. "What has happened?"

The man let out a loud and ugly laugh.

"Her asks what's happened!" he said to the other men. "Shall we tell her? Perhaps she'd like to drink the wine that comes from 'em!"

He spoke in an ugly jeering voice and with a violence that made Syrilla want to shrink away from him.

"I can see there is a disease," she said. "Surely the vines should have been uprooted and burnt."

She spoke seriously but her words were greeted by jeers and cat-calls.

"If the *Duchesse* knows what should be done, why don't she tell the *Duc* and get him to give an order?"

There was a burst of voices in answer to this, and in the medley of sound Syrilla realised that this was what they had wanted the *Duc* to see, and this in fact was their grievance.

She wondered why the diseased vines had been left, but felt it would not be safe to say too much without having a real knowledge of what had happened.

A little way further on they reached the village, and now she could see the dilapidated condition of some of the houses.

From a distance they had seemed quite attractive, but now she could see holes in the roofs, windows hung with sacking, doors hanging askew from their hinges.

To watch them ride by a number of children came into the roadway, and one look at them told Syrilla what was wrong.

These people were starving!

The women's faces were grey and lined, the children's cheek-bones stood out, and their arms seemed to have no flesh on them.

They moved slowly past the houses and Syrilla had the feeling that the women in the doorways were too apathetic even to jeer at her or shout, as the men had done.

They had moved on a little way, when an elderly woman came running from one of the houses holding something in her arms.

The man leading Syrilla's horse by the bridle stopped, and the woman ran to the tall man who had spoken to her first and had been walking at her side.

She thrust out what she held in her arms towards him and looking down Syrilla saw that it was a baby —a very small baby with a wrinkled face and closed eyes, which must have just been born.

"Dead!" the woman shrieked. "Dead! And what do you expect with its mother without a bite to eat?"

The man stared for a moment at the dead child, then looked up at Syrilla.

"This is your doin'," he said. "Damn you—and damn all aristocrats! You've killed my son, and ye deserve to die!"

He almost spat the words at her, but Syrilla was not listening. She was looking at the baby and something stirred in her memory.

Without waiting for anybody to help her, she slipped down from her horse and going to the woman took the child in her arms.

She touched its face gently with her fingers and realised it was still warm, although certainly it looked dead.

Then she bent her head and did what she had seen Jacques do to the lamb.

She drew in her breath and blew as hard and as violently as she could through the baby's half-open lips.

Again she blew, giving her breath to the child.

Surprised into silence by her action, nobody moved or made any attempt to stop her.

Then as she breathed into the baby's mouth for the

fourth time one of its little hands stirred and a second later it gave a faint cry.

It was hardly audible, and yet those standing nearby heard it.

" 'Tis a miracle!"

It was the woman who had brought the child out from the cottage who whispered the words.

Then she gave a shrill shriek .

"The baby's alive! He's alive! 'Tis a miracle! God be praised! 'Tis a miracle!"

The child cried again and Syrilla drew the rough blanket in which he was wrapped closer and handed him back to the woman.

"Take him to his mother," she told her. "Tell her to keep him warm and feed him as soon as possible."

The woman gasped as if she had no words in which to reply. Then as she moved away Syrilla realised that everybody was staring at her incredulously.

For a moment it seemed as if they were all turned to stone. Then the women crossed themselves.

"That was my son!" the tall man beside Syrilla said unnecessarily.

"I think he will live," Syrilla said quietly. "Now, suppose you tell me what is wrong, and why the vines have died."

Chapter Five

Everybody talked at once and for a moment through the *mêlée* of sound Syrilla found it difficult to make sense of anything that was said.

Then she heard one word—*"Pyrale"*—and understood what had happened.

Her father had told her often enough of the menace that different moths were to the vines. He had explained to her about the *Cochylis,* or Night Moth, which was first found in Champagne in 1771.

The *Cochylis* strung threads of silk between the flowers and the buds, and late in the summer a second generation settled on the grapes, pricked them, and caused them to turn mouldy.

There was also the *Ver Blanc du Hanneton,* or White Moth of the Cockchafer, which was a particular enemy of the young wine and the grafted cuttings, besides the Red Cochenille moth, which laid its eggs in June and about a month later the young larvae started planting their suckers on the vine-shoots and the lower surface of the leaves.

All these were feared and dreaded by the wine-growers, but the *Pyrale,* a large moth whose body was yellow, with yellow wings, was perhaps the worst of all.

The *Comte* had told Syrilla that caterpillars hibernated in the bark of the branches all the winter to emerge in the spring. After spinning silken webs over the vine they proceeded to devour the buds, the young shoots, and the leaves.

Syrilla had listened and remembered what he had said. However, they had been fortunate at Monceau-sur-Indre and each year the grapes had ripened without mishap, making the *Comte* delighted with the wine he produced.

Now she realised she was seeing for herself the terrible devastation that the *Pyrale* moth could inflict on a vineyard.

She knew only too well that there was nothing that could be done about it, and the only remedy was for the vines to be dug up, the stumps removed with as many of the roots as would yield to pressure.

When a vine had been in the ground for perhaps twenty-five years, its roots were embedded in the soil and enormous strength was required to uproot the stump.

This meant, Syrilla knew, scooping out a great hole round the dead vine with pickaxes and crowbars, then hauling out the stump with a chain harnessed to a horse.

This was usually done as soon as the disease showed itself, and Syrilla could not understand why in this vineyard the vines had just been left and the men not ordered to remove them.

When she could make her voice heard she asked what the *Duc*'s Manager had done about the disease when they had reported it to him.

"He told us to find work elsewhere," an elderly man answered.

"And was that impossible?" Syrilla enquired.

"Who wants us at this time o' the year?" several of the men replied almost in unison. "In the harvest, yes—but we've been paid no money since the beginning of April."

Now Syrilla understood why they looked so ragged and why they all seemed to be suffering from starvation.

They explained graphically how at first they had their vegetables to eat while the men from the village searched far and wide over the countryside for other jobs.

Then in desperation, because the children were hungry, they killed their goats and chickens, which meant they had no milk or eggs.

Growing still more desperate, they decided when they heard of the *Duc*'s marriage that they must take violent action to acquaint him with their plight.

Syrilla gathered that it was the tall man whose son's life she had saved who had thought of kidnapping the *Duc* to make him aware of their problems.

They knew, she learnt, that when he was at the Château he rode every morning in the Park, and they decided to take him forcibly to their village to see the conditions for himself.

What they had not expected was to find Syrilla riding alone, and she had the feeling that while she was their hostage they were in fact a little embarrassed because she was a woman and not the man they wanted.

"The *Duc*'ll come to look for you," one man said gruffly, "he'll not want to lose his new wife so quickly."

There was some laughter at this, but it was not the jeering rudeness that Syrilla had heard when the men had brought her from the Park to their village.

Now they were looking at her not only with respect, but with something like awe, and she knew the fact that the women thought she had performed a miracle had also had an effect upon their husbands.

While she was talking to the men who were in a circle round her, the women and children had congregated on the outside.

Many of the children had sores and abrasions on their faces and hands and Syrilla knew this sprang from malnutrition.

Now she could understand the reason for their appearance.

There had been no money to buy thread to mend torn clothes, no money even for a nail with which to repair the broken shutters over the windows or to mend the hinges on the doors.

There was water in the stream, but she had the feeling that as the supply of food grew less the women became too weak even to wash their clothes, and their pale faces and the lack-lustre expression in their eyes confirmed this.

Finally, when she had heard all the men had to tell her, Syrilla said:

"It is not necessary for me to inform you that the *Duc* had no idea that this was happening on his Estate. I am absolutely certain it was not on his instructions that you were not paid your wages until you could find the employment."

Nobody spoke for the moment and she went on:

"I will return to the Château and ask *Monsieur le Duc* to come here and see for himself what you are suffering. I know that he will take steps immediately to put everything right."

As she spoke, she made to walk towards her horse, but the tall man barred her way.

"You'll not leave us," he said. "How do we know the *Duc*'ll not punish us for having taken you away? He might send his servants or even soldiers to turn us out of our houses, as his Agent has threatened to do."

He spoke truculently, and once again Syrilla felt a little tremor of fear as she saw that his words brought back expressions of ferocity and sullenness to the other men's faces.

With an effort she managed to smile at him.

"Very well," she replied. "I will wait here with you

while one of you takes a letter to *Monsieur le Duc* to explain what has happened to me. Will you please bring me paper and ink?"

This apparently involved some difficulty and while they were being found the women drew nearer, staring at Syrilla wide-eyed while one or two of them reached out tentatively to touch the skirts of her habit.

Then as she smiled at them they grew bolder and asked her help about their children.

Syrilla was sure there was little wrong except the lack of food, but she knew that until they had money there was no point in prescribing salves or lotions.

Instead she talked to them, telling them what she thought was a good diet for children provided that fresh vegetables and fruit were available and also the eggs and goats' cheese which was, she knew, an essential on a peasant's table in Touraine.

When writing-paper and an ink-pot containing very pale ink was brought and a quill pen which one of the men sharpened, she sat down in the chair they provided for her and wrote at a rough deal table which was badly in need of a scrub.

When she had written her note and folded it she said to the men:

"I think, to save time, one of you who can ride well —and I mean well—should take my horse to the Château."

"They'll accuse us of stealing it," was the answer.

"In which case ride as far as the wood," Syrilla said. "Tie the horse securely to a tree and walk the last part of the journey. When *Monsieur le Duc* has received the note the messenger can escort him back here."

The tall man looked doubtful.

"How do we know he'll come alone?" he asked. "If he brings men with fire-arms against us we'll fight, and you might get hurt."

"Monsieur le Duc will come alone because I have asked him to do so," Syrilla answered.

She knew they were sceptical. At the same time, there seemed to be no alternative to what she had suggested.

Three of the men said they were experienced riders and Syrilla chose the youngest of them. He was also the lightest and she had noticed him patting and making a fuss of her horse while she was writing the letter.

He mounted and rode off in silence and Syrilla knew, although the men sounded blustering and brave when they talked to her, that they were in fact extremely apprehensive at what would be the result of their action in kidnapping her.

To put them at their ease she sat down in the shade of a tree which grew in the centre of the village and began to talk with the women.

Soon they had seated themselves round her, many of them with their children in their arms.

Syrilla talked to them about her own childhood in Monceau-sur-Indre. She told them that her mother had died and how much she missed her.

She related too how she had first seen the *Duc* at the Tournament that had taken place at the Château when he was twenty-one.

Many of the women could remember the Tournament and they nodded agreement when she described what a magnificent spectacle it had been. Syrilla learnt that the old *Duc* had given every worker on the Estate a week's extra wages to celebrate his son's coming-of-age.

"Any of you who saw *Monsieur le Duc* then when he was dressed as a Knight will know that he would always champion the cause of justice," she said, "and that is why when he learns how you have suffered you need no longer be afraid that he will not right what is wrong."

* * *

The *Duc,* after seeking vainly for Syrilla in the Park, had returned to the Château to see if she had come back by a different route and he had missed seeing her.

"She is not here, *Monsieur,*" Pierre de Bethune told him.

"Then where can she be?" the *Duc* asked. "I cannot believe that she would go to the vineyards without me. In fact I rode through the woods and a little way into the fields, but there was no sign of her."

"You could not have missed *Madame* in her white riding-habit," Pierre de Bethune said.

The two men were standing on the steps of the Château, and all the time he was talking the *Duc*'s eyes had been searching the green Park expecting at any moment to see Syrilla come riding from between the trees.

"It seems extraordinary," Pierre de Bethune said. "You do not think there could have been an accident or the horse has bolted?"

"I have never known a woman who could ride as well as *Madame,*" the *Duc* interposed, "and if the horse had thrown her I cannot help feeling he would have returned to the stable."

"Yes, that is true," Pierre de Bethune agreed.

It was then that the *Duc* noticed a man come tramping through the great wrought-iron gates which stood at the entrance to the courtyard.

He looked at him indifferently. Then, as the man advanced towards the front door and did not turn off towards the back quarters as might have been expected, he waited, feeling in some strange way that this man was concerned with Syrilla.

As the man drew nearer to where the *Duc* was standing, Pierre de Bethune realised that he carried a note in his hand.

There was silence until the young man, thin and ragged, reached the foot of the steps, and looked up at the two gentlemen towering above him.

"Which of ye be the *Duc* de Savigne?" he asked.

The *Duc* took a step down towards him.

"I am!" he said sharply.

"Then this be for ye!" the man answered.

He thrust out the note as he spoke and the *Duc* took it from him.

He read it, and Pierre de Bethune, watching him closely, saw his lips tighten ominously.

"Where is *Madame la Duchesse?*" he asked harshly.

"She be wi' us at Tauxise," the man replied.

"What is it? What has happened?" Pierre de Bethune asked hastily, unable to control his curiosity.

The *Duc* handed him Syrilla's note and he read:

Monseigneur,

The People who tend one of Your Vineyards have been harshly and I feel unjustly treated since the Vines were devastated by the Pyrale Moth. They intended to bring You here to see for Yourself what They were Suffering. They have taken Me instead.

I have promised Them that as soon as You receive this You will come Alone and put things right. The Bearer of this note will show You the way.

I remain, Monseigneur,
Your affectionate and
admiring wife,
Syrilla.

"They are holding *Madame* as hostage!" Pierre de Bethune said hoarsely in a low voice.

The *Duc* turned to look at him and as the eyes of the two men met they both knew without words what the other feared.

The *Duc* snapped his fingers towards the groom who was standing holding the stallion that he had been riding until he returned to the Château.

The man moved forward.

"You must not go unaccompanied, *Monsieur*,"

Pierre de Bethune said in a low voice, "it might be dangerous!"

"You have read *Madame*'s note," the *Duc* replied. "She has asked me to come alone."

"She may have been forced to write it," Pierre de Bethune suggested.

"That is a possibility," the *Duc* agreed. "Nevertheless, I have no alternative but to obey her request."

"Let me send someone with you," Pierre de Bethune said, "or for God's sake at least go armed."

"I have a feeling that *Madame* trusts me to carry out her wishes exactly as she has expressed them," the *Duc* replied quietly.

"*Monsieur*—listen to me . . ." Pierre de Bethune begged, but already the *Duc* had swung himself into the saddle.

"Have I to wait for you, young man?" he asked the bearer of the note.

"I've a horse, *Monsieur le Duc*. I left it at the edge of the Park."

"Then run ahead and collect it," the *Duc* commanded.

The man started to run from the courtyard back into the Park and the *Duc* held his horse as he said to his Comptroller:

"Send for the Manager of the vineyard and have him here to await our return. I want an explanation of this—and it had better be a good one!"

"*Monsieur*, let me go with you," Pierre de Bethune begged.

The *Duc* looked down at him from the height his position in the saddle gave him.

"*Madame* wishes me to go alone, Pierre," he said. "I have a feeling that she is visualising me in the role of a White Knight, in which case I shall need no help in slaying the dragon!"

There was a note of light-hearted amusement in his

voice which surprised Pierre de Bethune and as the *Duc* rode away he stared after him in perplexity.

* * *

Syrilla had almost exhausted her fund of stories and was in fact finding that the hours she had been talking had made her throat very dry.

But she told herself she had no right to complain when she knew that many of the children, now that the excitement of her appearance was over, were whimpering with hunger.

She had also noticed that the men, sitting round and apparently keeping guard over her, were chewing pieces of wood as if the mere fact of having something in their mouths was a little compensation for the emptiness of their stomachs.

All the time she was talking she had been glancing towards the end of the village at the woods. She had been escorted along the side of them by the men who had brought her here.

She knew it was the way the *Duc* would come, and when finally she saw two horses silhouetted against the green trees she felt her heart give a leap of excitement.

She had known he would not fail her!

Yet at the same time she had been half-afraid that because people were so apprehensive of anything that appertained to a Revolutionary action, he might, despite her request, have brought a number of his grooms with him.

But there was no mistaking the *Duc*'s upright figure on the great black stallion, and she felt as if her love went out towards him in a great wave of warmth and adoration.

As Syrilla watched the *Duc* approach the village, so did everybody else.

He was riding fast, and now that he had been shown by his guide where Tauxise lay, he appeared to spur his horse forward and come towards them at a tremendous speed.

Slowly the men rose to their feet and the women and children did likewise. As the *Duc* reached the houses Syrilla moved swiftly towards him.

It seemed to her that he had eyes for no-one else, and he swung himself from the saddle, taking her outstretched hands in his and raising them one after another to his lips.

"You are all right?" he asked urgently.

"You have come! I knew you would come!" she cried.

"You asked me to come alone."

"I am grateful. You are needed here."

"What is wrong?"

Syrilla made a little gesture towards the vineyards.

"You can see for yourself."

"What is it?" the *Duc* asked.

"The *Pyrale* moth!"

At Syrilla's words the men who had apparently been speechless and spellbound at the *Duc*'s appearance found their voices.

"Yes—*Pyrale* moth!" the tall man said. "It's not our fault it's killed the vines, but because of it we've been left to starve! Starve, *Monsieur*! Look at our women, look at our children, look at us!"

The *Duc* looked round as he was asked to do.

"You have received no wages?" he enquired.

There was a roar of voices at this, all telling him how long they had been without money, how they had been forced to wander over the countryside in search of jobs which did not exist, and how they had returned to the village merely because there was nowhere else they could go.

The voices rose to a note of violence as the men explained their grievances and the manner in which they had been treated, but even so the *Duc* could hear Syrilla's voice as she said very softly:

"The children are starving. I managed to save one of them from dying, but others will die unless something is done—and quickly!"

The *Duc* held up his hand for silence and surprisingly he was obeyed.

"I have listened to your complaints," he said, "and I agree they are entirely justified. I will now give my orders to the men of Tauxise, and I expect them to be carried out."

It seemed to Syrilla that everybody held their breath as the *Duc* continued:

"You will pull up the vines immediately, clear the land, and plant, as is usual in such circumstances, potatoes and mustard. This work should take some months, but you are well aware that these vineyards will have to remain fallow for the next five years."

The *Duc* looked round at the men who were listening to him intently.

"I intend to discover during the next month or so whether it is best to remove this village completely and build you new houses on another part of my Estate, or whether it might not be reasonable to clear part of the woodland to the West and plant a new vineyard there."

He pointed as he spoke and went on:

"If the soil is good and the position gets the sun, I see no reason why the territory served by the village of Tauxise should not be extended."

There was a little gasp as the *Duc*'s words percolated the men's minds.

"We'd prefer that, *Monsieur*," the tall man said after a moment. "Most of us have lived here all our lives."

"We shall of course have to go into the problem thoroughly," the *Duc* said, "and I would appreciate your opinion as to whether the planting of such a vineyard is really worthwhile."

There was a little murmur at this, but it was a warm

one of approval, and very different from the mutterings Syrilla had heard before.

The *Duc*, looking at the women listening on the outside of the circle, said:

"I appreciate, as does my wife, *Madame la Duchesse,* that something must be done at once for the women and children—in fact for all of you. Your wages will be paid immediately and you will be fully compensated for the months during which you have received nothing.

"I intend to return to the Château now and order that goats and chickens are to be provided for the village from my own farm. There will also be grain and flour from my granaries so that you can start baking again."

This time the women cheered and because it was so spontaneous and at the same time so weak Syrilla felt the tears come into her eyes.

The *Duc* drew a purse from his pocket and said:

"I am afraid I carry little gold with me, but this should be enough to purchase a few commodities from the next village until I can send you everything I have promised. I shall not delay. It will be here this afternoon."

They cheered again and the *Duc* said:

"I think now it is time I took my wife home."

The men parted to let the *Duc* and Syrilla walk towards their horses, but many of the women went down on their knees to kiss the hem of her skirt as she passed by them.

Only as they reached the horses did the elderly woman who had brought out what she had thought was a dead baby on Syrilla's arrival at the village, come running from a house.

The baby was in her arms and he was crying loudly and angrily:

"Bless him, *Madame*," she said to Syrilla. "Bless the

child to whom you gave life. You are an angel come from God Himself!"

As she spoke the woman knelt down on the dusty road and held up the crying child.

For a moment Syrilla hesitated, then gently she put her hand on the baby's head.

"This child has already been blessed by God," she said. "It is not I who gave him life, but God, because life comes only from Him."

Everyone was listening and Syrilla still with her hand on the baby's head continued:

"May I suggest that you name this child after the man who has helped you and who I know will bring you good fortune for the future."

She smiled at the *Duc* as she spoke and added quietly but clearly:

"The name is Aristide!"

"It would be a very great honour, *Monsieur*," the father of the infant said.

"Then of course I am delighted that your son should be named after me," the *Duc* replied.

He picked up Syrilla in his arms as he spoke and lifted her into the saddle. Then as he mounted his own horse he said to the villagers:

"The quicker we return the quicker you shall have the things I have promised you."

He turned his horse as he spoke and Syrilla followed him. For a little way the women ran beside her, touching her skirt, calling out their thanks. Then at the end of the village they dropped behind and Syrilla waved to them until she and the *Duc* reached the woods.

They rode for a little until the *Duc* asked:

"You were not frightened?"

"Only at first," Syrilla confessed. "But after I saved the baby's life I knew they would not hurt me."

"Tell me how you did it."

She told him how she had seen her father's shepherd save the lamb's life and how the Cardinal had said that life came from God, but sometimes it could be transmitted to others.

"I have never heard of anything so extraordinary!" the *Duc* exclaimed.

"They meant to kidnap you and threaten you," Syrilla told him in a low voice, "but I explained that you could not have been aware what was happening to them."

The *Duc* was silent for a moment, and then said:

"Nevertheless, you blame me for letting such things occur on my Estate."

Syrilla did not answer.

"Tell me the truth," the *Duc* insisted mockingly.

She had the feeling he was almost forcing her to blame him.

"I understand, *Monseigneur*," she said at length, "how you have dedicated yourself to helping the poor and unfortunate of Paris; but you are needed here too, and these are your people."

The *Duc* opened his lips as if he would reply. Then he spurred his horse on a little faster and there was a look on his face that she did not understand.

When they arrived at the Château, Pierre de Bethune was waiting for them.

He ran down the steps with an expression of intense relief on his face.

"You are all right, *Madame?*" he enquired.

"Quite all right," Syrilla answered, "but *Monsieur* has a great many things which he wishes to be done at once."

She paused, and added:

"Please hurry with them . . . it is urgent . . . very urgent!"

She knew that Pierre de Bethune would obey her request, and she walked into the house, leaving the *Duc* giving sharp, staccato orders which she had the impression astonished not only his Comptroller but also his servants.

She felt a little tired as she went upstairs to her room.

The maids helped her change from her riding-habit into a thin gown and she went downstairs knowing she was very hungry but feeling somehow ashamed when she thought of how the villagers must have suffered at being so long with little or no food.

The *Duc* was waiting for her in the Salon and when she entered he put a glass of wine into her hand.

"Drink this," he said. "I feel you need it."

"I am very thirsty," Syrilla admitted.

Then as if she could not prevent herself from asking the question she enquired:

"Has everything gone to the village?"

"Not everything," the *Duc* answered. "It will take time to get the goats and chickens there, but to bridge the delay I have already sent to Tauxise a considerable amount of food such as hams, fish, and bread from our own larders."

"Thank you . . . thank you, I knew you would do something like that," Syrilla cried.

She thought the *Duc* was looking at her with a strange expression in his eyes and after a moment she asked:

"Have you seen the Manager of the vineyards?"

"He is waiting for me," the *Duc* replied. "It will do him good to cool his heels. By now he must know what has happened."

"You intend to dismiss him?"

The *Duc* paused for a moment before he said:

"I am wondering if he has sinned more against these people than I have. As you so rightly said, Syrilla, they are my responsibility."

"He was inhuman," Syrilla said, "and that is something you could never be to anyone!"

She thought the *Duc* was about to say something, but at that moment luncheon was announced and he waited for her to lead the way into the Dining-Room.

Despite Syrilla's protests the *Duc* insisted after their meal that she should lie down.

"If you are not tired you should be," he said. "You have been through an experience which would be trying and indeed frightening to anyone."

"I want to be . . . with you," Syrilla protested.

"I am going to interview my Manager and Agent," the *Duc* said. "I have a suspicion that this meeting will not be a very pleasant one, and quite frankly I would prefer you not to be there."

"Then I will lie down," Syrilla agreed, "but please, *Monseigneur*, may we go to the vineyards tomorrow? I was so looking forward to seeing them when I was with you."

"Then we will visit them tomorrow," the *Duc* promised.

He saw the light in her eyes and told himself it was useless for him to think of returning to Paris at the moment when there was so much to be done here on his Estates.

Why, he asked savagely, could they not have been administered as competently as they had been in his father's time?

Even as he asked the question he knew the answer and was afraid to express it even to himself.

* * *

Syrilla lay down in the beautiful bed-room which had been occupied over the centuries by many Queens of France.

She loved the pale blue brocade panelling on the walls, the painted ceiling depicting Venus surrounded by cupids, in soft pinks and blues that were echoed in the Aubusson carpet on the floor.

There was a faint breeze billowing the silk curtains and she felt almost as if it brought the sound of music to her ears.

"I am happy," she told herself, 'far happier than I imagined it possible to be, and it is all because of *Monseigneur*. He is so wonderful!"

She thought of what had happened that morning and added:

"It is only because he has been away in Paris that things have gone wrong here at Savigne."

She said a little prayer that the *Duc* would find so much to do here in his own home and on his own lands that he would not wish to return to Paris too soon.

"They will miss him," she told herself, "but he is needed here—desperately needed!"

She knew it was not only the villagers of Tauxise and other places who needed the *Duc*. There was a yearning within herself that they should be together in the peace and tranquillity of Touraine.

Syrilla was afraid of Paris; she thought how lost, inexperienced, and ignorant she would appear in the sophisticated, brilliant Society in which the *Duc* undoubtedly moved and of which she had no knowledge whatsoever.

Had her mother been alive, she thought, she would not have been so afraid, but her father had never been concerned with Society and she was sure there were a hundred pitfalls and a thousand mistakes she would make unknowingly with no-one to guide her.

"Please, God," she prayed, "Let *Monseigneur* wish to stay here where we are so happy and it is so beautiful . . . and there is no-one to come between us."

She did not know really what she meant by her last words, and yet instinctively she knew that her contentment was menaced in some strange and unaccountable way.

She had no idea what it might be: perhaps the *Duc*'s pre-occupation with the work to which he had dedicated himself, perhaps the people with whom he associated.

She could not formulate any constructive idea of what might be waiting in the future.

She only knew it was like a cloud looming upon the horizon and that it was definitely there, even though the *Duc* had not spoken again of leaving the Château.

"I love him! Oh, God, I love him with every thought and every breath I draw," Syrilla prayed. "Make him love me a little. Make him want to be with me and I will not ask for more."

She prayed intensely. At the same time, she was in fact a little tired and after a time she fell asleep.

She awoke because her maids came in with her bath and she realised to her surprise that it was time to dress for dinner.

Glancing at the clock, Syrilla felt that she had wasted several precious hours in sleeping when she might have been with the *Duc*.

He would have finished his interviews with the Manager and the Agent and perhaps they could have walked together in the garden or sat on the terrace, and she could have talked to him as she loved to do.

"Quickly, quickly, Marie!" she said to her maid. "Bring me my prettiest gown! Then I will go downstairs. *Monsieur Le Duc* always changes early, and I want to be with him."

Nevertheless, it took a little time to bathe in the rose-scented water and to be dressed in one of the beautiful gowns which the *Duchesse* had ordered from Paris.

It was a very pretty dress of white tulle trimmed with blue ribbons and little posies of pink rose-buds.

As her maid fastened it at the back, Syrilla hoped the *Duc* would admire her in it. She knew that always when she appeared she searched his eyes for just a glint of admiration that she was sure was sometimes there.

There was a cluster of tiny pink roses to wear at the back of her head and she clasped round her neck a diamond chain that had been one of her wedding presents.

From it hung a locket in the shape of a heart and Syrilla decided that when she knew the *Duc* a little better she would beg him to have a miniature painted so that she could wear it in the locket which would always be close to her.

Finally she was ready, and thanking her maid she hurried from the room onto the wide landing off which led the Grand Staircase which ended in the big marble Hall.

Because she was in such a hurry to be with the *Duc,* Syrilla ran down the staircase and seemed almost to fly across the Hall towards the Salon where she thought he would be waiting.

As the flunkey opened the door for her and she passed into the room she saw with a sudden feeling of disappointment that the Salon was empty.

Then she realised that the *Duc* was outside on the terrace and she moved across the carpet towards the open window.

She had almost reached it when she heard footsteps outside and saw Pierre de Bethune approach the *Duc,* who was standing against the balustrade looking out over the lake below.

"*Monsieur,*" his voice was urgent. "The newspapers have just arrived from Paris and they say that Astrid was released from prison three days ago!"

There was a note in Pierre de Bethune's voice that brought Syrilla to a standstill. She stood just inside the open window of the Salon and because she remembered the name she could not help listening.

"Astrid?" the *Duc* asked. "Then his sentence must have been completed. It was for eight years, I remember."

"He is free, *Monsieur*, and you must be very careful!"

The *Duc* did not reply and after a moment his Comptroller went on:

"You know he swore to kill you!"

"That was a long time ago, Pierre. His temper has doubtless cooled while he has been in prison."

"I should think that is most unlikely," Pierre de Bethune insisted. "He was an animal, *Monsieur*, a dangerous, ferocious animal!"

He paused and Syrilla knew that he shivered as he finished:

"I can still hear him shouting at you from the Dock. He sounded almost insane."

"He was insane," the *Duc* agreed. "But now he is free, Pierre, and there is nothing I can do about it."

"Except take care of yourself."

"What do you suggest I do?" the *Duc* asked.

It seemed to Syrilla there was a note of amusement in his voice.

"I shall give instructions immediately to double the night-guards in the Château," Pierre de Bethune said. "I shall also have men and dogs patrolling the grounds. They will be armed, and, on my instructions, *Monsieur*, they will shoot the moment they see Astrid."

"I think you are over-dramatising the situation, Pierre," the *Duc* said. "Besides, if he strangles me it would perhaps be poetic justice."

"You should not talk like that, *Monsieur*," Pierre de Bethune said sharply, "and I beg of you, for the sake of *Madame la Duchesse*, not to do anything foolhardy."

As if she could not listen any longer without taking part in the conversation, Syrilla walked onto the terrace.

At the sound of her footsteps both men turned to look at her.

She ran towards the *Duc*.

"I overheard what you were saying," she said. "Oh, *Monseigneur*, you are in danger!"

"Pierre was exaggerating," the *Duc* said calmly. "I

am in no danger, Syrilla. This man has spent eight years in prison. He is not likely to wish to languish there for another eight!"

"B-but he . . . threatened you," Syrilla said in a low voice.

"Men say many things when they are convicted of murder," the *Duc* remarked coolly.

"Why . . . why was he not . . . guillotined?" Syrilla asked in a low voice.

There was a moment's pause.

"It was a *Crime Passionel* and the jury are usually sentimental about such a situation."

Syrilla would have spoken but he interrupted:

"I have no wish to speak about it any longer. You would not have heard of this if Pierre had not come cackling to me like a mother hen. Forget it, Syrilla. Savigne is the safest place in the world as far as I am concerned and we can leave ourselves in Pierre's good hands."

He looked at his Comptroller meaningfully as he spoke and Pierre de Bethune knew he was dismissed.

"Your pardon, *Monsieur*, for mentioning the matter," he said. "I am well aware that I was unduly anxious."

He bowed as he moved away, and Syrilla looked up at the *Duc*.

"Please, *Monseigneur*," she said, "you must be very careful. If anything should happen to you . . . my whole world would come to an end and I would . . . want to die!"

Chapter Six

When dinner was finished and they had moved into the Salon, Syrilla said to the *Duc*:

"Please tell me, *Monseigneur,* what you have done."

He knew to what she referred, and sitting down in a chair he said:

"I dismissed the Manager of the vineyard and my Agent. They were both well aware of what was happening at Tauxise."

"I am so glad," Syrilla said. "I cannot bear to think of how those poor people must have suffered, and there might be others like them."

"I will take good care that this never occurs again," the *Duc* said firmly. "The Manager came to us from Bordeaux with a big reputation, but I think in future I would be wise to entrust my vines to a local man who understands Touraine and our particular requirements."

"Papa always says that people who understand our local difficulties are better than those who come from other parts of France."

"Your father is right," the *Duc* agreed, "and I hope in future, Syrilla, you will not be anxious about anything which is happening on the Estate."

There was silence and looking at her expressive face he knew that something was worrying her.

"What is it?" he asked.

She hesitated before she answered. Then she said in a low voice.

"I would not wish to make . . . trouble."

"I think you have something to tell me," the *Duc* said, "and I want you to be frank with me, Syrilla."

Still she hesitated, and he went on:

"After all, you are my wife, and anything in the house or on the Estate that concerns me also concerns you and is in part your responsibility."

"I had forgotten that," she said simply.

"It is true," the *Duc* replied, "and now tell me what is worrying you."

"I know that I should not . . . listen to servants' gossip," Syrilla began in a low voice, "but they always talk . . . including, of course, my maid Marie when she is dressing me."

"I can understand that," the *Duc* smiled. "Gustave, my valet, often lectures me!"

"Marie's brother works in the stables," Syrilla said, "and when you are not here the horses are often not . . . exercised and sometimes . . . neglected."

"What do you mean—neglected?" the *Duc* asked sharply.

"I understand your Head-groom is very old," Syrilla replied, "and in the winter he suffers from rheumatism. He therefore leaves everything to the under-groom, who is a lazy man, and at times the horses are skimpily fed and do not have water."

Syrilla did not look at the *Duc* as she spoke. She was embarrassed at telling him that such things were happening, because she felt that everything that concerned him should be perfect in every respect.

The *Duc* rose to his feet.

"Curse it!" he said. "Why can I not be served properly?"

He sounded so angry that after a moment's hesitation Syrilla said:

"Mama said once that servants are like actors. They need applause, or, in other words, to be praised; otherwise they feel that if they do not have an appreciative audience it is not worth giving a good performance!"

The *Duc* walked to the mantelshelf and stood with his back to her.

"What you are saying once again," he said, "is that my stables, like my vineyards, need my personal supervision."

"I did not wish to . . . upset you by telling you . . . these things," Syrilla replied, "but of course that is the truth. If the gardens look lovely and there is no-one to say so, why should the gardeners take so much trouble?"

She paused and continued in a hesitating voice:

"If your horses are not in . . . fine fettle and you are not . . . here to ride . . . them, who is to . . . care?"

She could not see the *Duc*'s face, but she was sure he was scowling and after a moment she pleaded:

"Please do not be . . . angry with me for saying . . . this, but you told me to be . . . frank with . . . you."

"I want you always to tell me what you think is the truth," the *Duc* said, "and I believe you are always truthful, Syrilla."

"Of course," she answered, "and you know I would never lie to you of all people."

"You are unlike most women I know," he said cynically.

"That is not a compliment," Syrilla replied. "I realise how . . . inadequate and . . . dull I must be compared with the . . . brilliantly intelligent and . . . beautiful women you know in Paris."

There was a wistfulness in her voice that was somehow pathetic. The *Duc* seemed about to say something, then changed his mind.

"You have had a long day, Syrilla," he said, "and

you must be tired. I suggest you go to bed and we will talk about this in the morning."

"I would rather . . . stay and talk to . . . you," she said quickly.

"Shall I say that I have a lot to think about?" he said. "What has happened today has given me a great deal to consider and has perhaps turned my feet in a direction they have never travelled before."

Syrilla did not understand, but she was too sensitive to press the point that she wanted to stay with him when she realised the *Duc* wished her to go.

Instead she rose to her feet to stand beside him.

"I would like to tell you how . . . proud I was when I saw you riding into the village this morning," she said. "I told the villagers you would solve all their . . . problems, but I know they did not really . . . believe me."

She paused and her eyes looked up at him admiringly as she went on:

"But you did come! You seemed to have a shining light about you and I knew that you would make them happy again."

"I told Pierre that you intended me to slay the dragon," the *Duc* said with a twist of his lips.

"That is what you did," Syrilla smiled. "But I think, *Monseigneur,* there are other dragons that also require your attention."

She looked into his eyes as she spoke and now it seemed as if neither of them could look away.

Something Syrilla did not understand passed between them; she felt that her heart was beating frantically and had risen into her throat while her lips parted because it was hard to breathe.

Just for a moment it seemed as if everything vanished except the *Duc* and they were alone on a high place in the sunshine.

Then he said almost curtly:

"Go to bed, Syrilla, and leave me to my thoughts."

He raised her hand to his lips and she curtseyed, but as she went from the room she was conscious only of the touch of his mouth against her skin.

* * *

Marie helped Syrilla to undress, then when she got into bed Marie blew out the candles and would have left the room but Syrilla said:

"Pull back the curtains over the centre window, Marie. It is still not too dark and I want to watch the stars come out. Besides, it is very hot."

"I'll do that, *Madame*," Marie answered, "but I hope the light doesn't wake you too early."

"I wish to wake early," Syrilla replied, "there is so much to do."

She knew what she was really saying was that she wanted to be with the *Duc*.

When she was alone Syrilla stared out at the translucent sky deepening to sable overhead where the first evening stars were like tiny diamonds.

Soon she knew they would be reflected in the lake and she wondered if any place in the world could be as beautiful as the Château Savigne.

"Or any man so magnificent as its owner!" she whispered.

She thought of the strange feeling she had felt in her heart when she had looked into his eyes as they had said good-night.

It was the truth when she had told him that, as he rode into the village where she was waiting so anxiously for him, it had seemed as if he was enveloped in a shining light.

She had thought for a moment that he was in the silver armour he had worn when she first saw him in the Tournament.

She had loved him then, and now she realised it had been a child's love: the adoration she had felt all through the following years had been for a mythical being, a god-like creature who was not really flesh and blood.

Now she knew that the *Duc* was a man and she faced the fact that in the last few days her love for him had changed.

She had thought on her wedding day that she would go on worshipping him as the embodiment of all that was noble and fine, but somehow, imperceptibly, her love had changed until now when she saw him her heart leapt in a very different manner.

When he kissed her hand she had known irrepressibly that what she yearned for was for him to kiss her lips.

"I love him! I love him!" she told herself. "And I think the love I have for him now is that of a woman."

She found herself pulsating with strange sensations she had never known before, and because they were disturbing and a little frightening she rose from the bed to go to the *Prie-Dieu*.

She knelt down on the velvet cushion and put her hands together, palm to palm as she had done ever since childhood, bent her head, and began the prayers she had learnt at her mother's knee.

The conventional Hail Mary was said, and then she prayed passionately to God to make the *Duc* love her because he needed and wanted her.

"Make him forget his other love," she prayed. "Make him think of me. Make him love me a little, just a little, as a man loves a woman."

She had a feeling that perhaps she was wrong to ask such a thing, and yet her whole being yearned for the *Duc* in a manner that was quite different from any emotion she had ever felt before.

Her body ached for him, her lips were soft and tender because they craved for his, and she knew that her real idea of Heaven would be to feel his arms round her.

"I love him! Oh, God, I love him!" she said. "Can love ever be wrong if it comes from You and is a part of You? I love him so much that he fills my whole world and there is nothing else but him."

How long she prayed Syrilla had no idea, but her feelings were so intense that she felt God must hear them and that she poured her very life into her prayers.

Finally, when she felt almost exhausted by the effort that had involved every nerve in her body as well as every thought in her mind, she repeated the Gloria, as her mother had taught her to do to end her prayers.

As she crossed herself she heard a sound at the window.

As she said the last "Amen" she vaguely thought perhaps it was a bird or a bat seeking entry into the room.

She turned round, still kneeling on the *Prie-Dieu,* to see something so strange that for the moment she could not think what it was.

Half blocking out the stars which now vividly filled the sky outside was a dark shadow.

As she stared at it, wondering what it could be, it seemed to come lower and lower until when it reached the sill the sky was almost completely obscured by it.

Bewildered, but for the moment unafraid, Syrilla rose slowly to her feet. Then the shadow came lower still and she realised that silhouetted against the stars she could see the body of a man!

With a sudden tension she remembered who it was and the danger it implied!

There was no need to ask who was entering the Château in such a manner, who the shadowy figure sought and why.

With a cry of terror that came from her very heart she ran towards him.

* * *

The *Duc* sat for a long time in the Salon, until finally as if he had found no conclusion to his thoughts he went upstairs to bed.

His valet was waiting for him, and sensing that his master had no wish to chatter, Gustave helped him undress in silence and said nothing until he murmured respectfully from the door:

"Bonsoir, Monsieur le Duc."

The *Duc* did not bother to reply.

He left the candelabra alight and got into bed almost petulantly as if he defied himself to sleep. He knew even as he lay back against the pillows that he would not be able to do so.

He had wanted to think of his future plans tonight, but instead he had been haunted, despite every resolution not to think of him, by Astrid.

The scene in the dock kept coming back to him as vividly as if it had happened yesterday rather than nine years ago.

The *Duc* could hear his voice shouting obscenities, cursing him with every filthy oath that was used in the gutters of Paris and swearing that sooner or later he would kill him with his bare hands.

"You will die, my fine *Duc!*" he yelled as the Gendarmes dragged him away to the cells. "You will die as Zivana did, black in the face and gasping for air! You will die and your soul will rot in hell!"

It was the climax to a trial which had been horrible and humiliating, and which the *Duc* knew had changed his whole character and personality.

He had hoped he would be able to forget, and in his efforts to find forgetfulness he had plumbed the very depths of depravity and wallowed in filth which would have made any normal man's mind find ordinary thought an impossibility.

But he had been unable to erase from his consciousness and from his memory what he had learnt at the trial.

He remembered the first time he had seen Jules Astrid.

The man had been performing in one of the "turns" which took place in the Théâtre des Variétés, where Zivana was appearing in the Ballet.

The *Duc* had thought at the time that Astrid was a rather magnificent figure of a man and he learnt later that he had played many different parts in his life.

In his desire to reach the stage, Astrid had been an assistant to a lion-tamer in a Circus and he had also been an acrobat.

It was because of his fine looks that he was offered a small part by a touring company in the provinces, and as it had always been his ambition to become an actor he had left the Circus to tour in France.

In course of time he played every male part in the company's repertoire, until eventually he became the lead.

A talent-spotter from Paris noticed him and he was offered a leading part opposite an actress who had achieved fame but was now in fact too old to hold the audience in a full-length play.

She could still however command a large salary for a sketch in one of the many Theatres of Variety. The sketch received excellent reviews and she and Jules Astrid sometimes gave two or three performances at different theatres in one evening.

Although they played in the same theatre, the *Duc* had no idea that Zivana and Astrid had ever met.

Not until the Trial did he realise that the secret of what they felt for each other had not only been kept from him but also from the elderly actress.

She was insanely jealous and expected her leading man not only to play the part of lover on the stage but also in her private life.

Almost as if he were watching a play portrayed in his bed-room, the *Duc* could see Jules Astrid acting his part, commanding the applause of every woman in the audience, then as the Judge passed sentence, see his face contorted with rage, shouting and screaming at him like a wild animal.

"I will not think about him—I will not!" the *Duc* told himself.

But he thought how often he had tried to thrust such memories away from him, turning in his extremity to drink and women, to the orgies that had taken place in his house in Paris, to the excesses which made many of his closest friends turn from him in disgust.

Now when he had thought he had almost forgotten Astrid's existence, the strangler had come back to haunt him.

Actually he was not afraid of what the actor might do to him physically. He could not believe that in a trial of strength he would not emerge the victor.

There was, of course, always the chance, as Pierre de Bethune feared, that Astrid might shoot him in a crowd or knife him in the back when he was least expecting it.

But there was no defence against such an attack, unless he committed himself into a prison where he could be guarded day and night.

"If he kills me what would it matter?" the *Duc* asked himself. Then surprisingly he knew he did not wish to die.

After the Trial and the shock it had been to him, he wanted, if not to end his life, at least to change it completely.

If he had died in the process he knew that he would not have cared.

And yet now, astonishingly, he wanted to live.

Life had never seemed precious to him before. He had never thought it to be of any particular consequence.

But if he had to live, he had thought, he would enjoy himself and be damned to everyone else. Yet he wondered now in the darkness of his bed-room if the life he had led had brought him any enjoyment.

Had not some part of him always felt disgusted at the depravity to which he had sunk?

Had the bitterness and cynicism that invaded his mind, to the point when looking back he thought that he must have been at times a little mad, brought him anything but a sense of humiliation?

"Why should I think like this?" the *Duc* asked.

Why should the thought of Astrid being freed from prison bring back the misery and revulsion that he had felt after the Trial?

And yet it was hard to compare what he had felt then with what he felt now.

'I am older, I have no ideals left to be smashed, and no standards to lower,' the *Duc* thought savagely.

Yet now he wanted to live.

Quite suddenly it seemed to him that he had wasted the last nine years when there were so many other things he might have done with his time and money.

It was a thought that made him rise from his bed to pull back the curtains and look out the window into the night.

He realised as he did so that he had not really looked at the lake and the gardens of the Château in starlight since he was a boy.

Then it had seemed to him something so lovely, so mystical, so ethereal that his whole being had gone out in a desire to be part of it.

At the same time, he had the feeling of intense pride that this was his Kingdom, his possession, and he was a part of Savigne just as its history was a part of him.

He could see the stars reflected in the lake, a shimmer of silver on the still water, and he could see the great trees in the Park silhouetted against the sky.

There was the fragrance of flowers on the air, and he thought he detected the scent of Night-Stock, which was one of his mother's favourite flowers.

When he had gone to see the *Duchesse Dourairière* in the afternoon he had known, although she was too tactful to say so, how thrilled she was that he was still at the Château and had not returned to Paris as he had intended to do.

For the first time since boyhood there had been no need for words between them; for they had each known what the other was thinking.

"You have made me very happy, Aristide," his mother said softly.

The Doctor had told the *Duc* he was not to tire her and had warned him not to stay too long.

"*Madame la Duchesse* is better in health than I have known her to be for some time, but it would be a great mistake for her to become overtired."

"I will come and see you tomorrow, Mama," the *Duc* said, and had known by the sudden light in her eyes that that was what she wanted to hear.

He kissed her hand and felt her fingers tighten for a moment on his.

"God bless you, my dearest," she whispered.

Although he told himself it was absurd when he went from her room, he felt as if he had indeed been blessed.

The idea suddenly came to him that if anyone could save him from being haunted by Astrid it would be his mother and Syrilla.

It would be their prayers that would prove a barrier between him and the demons that jeered at him and the ghosts which had haunted him for so long.

Then he told himself that even prayer could not save him from physical danger.

Then suddenly he had an acute feeling that danger was very near.

He could not explain it to himself, but it was there almost like a tingling, not so much in his mind as at the end of his fingers and at the back of his neck.

There was danger—a danger which was coming nearer—danger which threatened him physically.

It was so intense that the *Duc* turned from the window to open a drawer in the chest that stood beside his canopied bed.

It was a beautiful chest of rosewood inlaid with ivory and was one of a pair that were very appropriate to the *Chambre du Roi.*

Lying in the top drawer was a loaded pistol.

The *Duc* had mocked at himself for doing so, but he had loaded it when he came up to bed after Pierre de Bethune had told him that Astrid was now free.

Yet how could any man, however fanatical his desire to murder, break through the defences with which the *Duc* knew his Comptroller had surrounded the house?

He had heard the tramp of the reinforced night-watchmen making their rounds. He knew that out in the grounds the game-keepers and the foresters had been given a rota by which they would patrol in three-hour shifts the gardens, the Park, and the woodlands.

"The whole thing is hysterical!" the *Duc* said scathingly. "Pierre is just an old man and I am a fool to listen to him."

But however contemptuous he might be, he knew the feeling of danger was still there.

It seemed to loom nearer and nearer, and now as if he could not help himself the *Duc* opened the connecting door into the passage which led to Syrilla's room.

"I must think of her safety, if not for my own," he told himself as an excuse for his own fears.

But there was no sound, and he thought he was just being nonsensical and the sooner he returned to bed the better.

"If I am going to feel like this every night," he told himself, "I shall go completely crazy!"

He stepped back into his own room and began to pull the communicating door to. As he did so, he heard Syrilla scream.

It took the *Duc* only a few seconds to run down the corridor to the door into Syrilla's room and as he reached it he heard her scream again.

He flung open her door and heard her cry frantically:

"You shall not hurt *Monseigneur!* You shall not kill him!"

He could see in the darkness a white patch which was Syrilla's nightgown as she struggled with someone big and dark against a background of stars.

It was easy for the *Duc* to perceive the outline of a man's head and shoulders against the sky and to be aware that he was struggling with Syrilla.

Instinctively he knew, with a terror which pierced him like a knife, that Astrid's hands were at Syrilla's throat.

"Die! Die as Zivana died!" he heard the murderer say in a voice that was like the snarl of a wild animal.

With the accuracy of an outstanding marksman the *Duc* shot him through the forehead.

Astrid fell backwards, his body thudding noisily to the floor, and the *Duc* picked up Syrilla from where she had collapsed at his feet.

It was impossible to see her clearly, but his arms lifted her from the carpet and he carried her from the room without even a glance towards the man he had killed.

She was very light and he held her close against him as he moved slowly down the connecting passage and into his bed-room.

He carried her to his bed and set her down against the pillows, and as her head lolled back against them he wondered with a sudden constriction of his heart if she was dead.

The marks of Astrid's fingers were on her neck, her eyes were closed, and he thought with a sudden terror that they were growing black as would happen if he had strangled her.

Frantically the *Duc* dragged at the bell-pull, then went back to kneel beside the bed and put his ear against Syrilla's breast.

Her heart was beating; he could hear it and knew she was alive, if nothing else.

He pulled the velvet counterpane over her, then knelt down looking at her for a long moment, before he rose to his feet to fling open the door to the corridor, intending to shout for help.

But at that moment he saw his valet, hastily buttoning his coat, come running towards him.

"Send for a Physician immediately!" the *Duc* cried, "and tell *Monsieur* de Bethune to come here to me with all possible speed!"

The sharpness of his voice and the abruptness with which he spoke made the valet turn immediately and run back the way he had come, but before he was halfway down the corridor Pierre de Bethune appeared.

"What is the matter?" he asked, as he moved towards the *Duc*. "I thought I heard a shot."

"You did!" the *Duc* replied briefly. "I have killed Astrid! He was in *Madame*'s bed-room."

"How was that possible?" Pierre de Bethune gasped.

"I think he must have come down from the roof on a rope," the *Duc* answered. "We might have remembered that he was an acrobat!"

"My God!" Pierre de Bethune exclaimed.

The *Duc* was speaking over his shoulder as he was returning to his bed-room.

"And *Madame?*" Pierre de Bethune asked.

He followed the *Duc* and saw Syrilla lying in the huge bed.

"He was attempting to strangle her!" the *Duc* explained.

"Attempting!"

Pierre de Bethune said the words almost under his breath; for in the candlelight Syrilla's cheeks were very white and her fair hair seemed to frame her face like a halo.

Just as the *Duc* had done, he knelt beside her and taking her wrist in his fingers felt for her pulse.

"She is alive!" he said.

But he too could see the scarlet marks of the murderer's hands on her white throat, and as he turned to meet the *Duc*'s eyes they were both thinking of the brain damage that might have been inflicted.

The *Duc* picked up a candelabrum and carried it round the velvet curtains of the bed to look more closely at Syrilla's face.

He had thought in his first panic that her eye-lids were growing black, but now he realised it had only been a shadow.

There was no darkness beneath them, and he gave a sigh of relief that seemed to come from the very depths of his being.

He put the candelabrum down again and said:

"Find out if they have already sent a groom for the Physician, and make quite certain that devil is dead. I think I shot him through the forehead."

Pierre de Bethune did not speak. He merely rose to his feet and went through the connecting door into Syrilla's bed-room.

The *Duc* knelt down again at Syrilla's side, and after a few moments he saw her eye-lids flicker.

"Syrilla!"

His voice was unexpectedly low and hoarse.

It seemed for a moment that she could not focus her eyes, and as he waited almost breathlessly for her response to his call she saw his face and a faint smile touched her lips.

She tried to speak and failed. Then as a little wavering hand crept towards her neck the *Duc* said:

"Do not speak. That fiend has hurt your neck, but if you understand what I say to you just try to nod your head."

Her eyes were on his face as he asked:

"Are you in pain?"

Almost imperceptibly she shook her head and as the *Duc* realised that his fears of brain damage were groundless he took her hand and kissed it.

"Lie still," he said. "I have sent for the Doctor. He will be here as quickly as possible. You must not try to move—it has been a great shock but it is all over."

He saw that she was trying to speak and knew without being told what she asked.

"I am safe," he said, his voice was very tender. "You were trying to save me, Syrilla, and you succeeded! I heard you scream and as I came into your room I saw you trying to protect me. I shot him, but not before he tried to strangle you."

He saw that she understood what he was saying. At the same time, the marks on her neck seemed to deepen and he felt she must be in some pain.

"If only I knew what to give you," the *Duc* said, "but I feel it would hurt you to drink."

Syrilla's fingers tightened on his and again he knew that all she really wanted was that he should be beside her and to be able to hold on to him.

"You are safe," the *Duc* said. "Safe now and forever!"

It was what she wanted to hear and again she gave him a little smile.

Then his lips were on her hand, lingering on the softness of her skin, kissing it again and again with a relief that he felt could only be expressed by some form of endearment.

* * *

Syrilla awoke to find the sunshine creeping golden into the room through the sides of the curtains and she thought that it must be very late in the day.

The events of the night came back to her and she

remembered vaguely the Doctor coming and giving her something to drink. It had been unpleasant but it had sent her into a deep sleep.

Now she realised she was not in her own room but in the *Duc*'s.

She could see in the dim light the huge carved gold pelmets above the three windows and the lofty impressive furniture very unlike the delicately carved pieces in her own room.

Gradually the events of what had happened came back to her. She remembered trying to prevent Astrid from attacking the *Duc* and feeling his fingers hard and frightening round her neck.

It had been a crazy thing to do, she thought, to try to prevent a large man from killing the *Duc* when she was weaponless and wearing nothing but a nightgown.

But she had been obsessed only with the idea of saving the man she loved and had not for a moment counted the cost to herself.

Only when she thought she was dying and felt the breath being choked out of her did she send a despairing, wordless cry to the *Duc* to save her.

And he saved her!

Vaguely as she fell into a deep unconsciousness she had heard a pistol-shot and knew in her heart who had fired it.

Then she had found him kneeling beside her, his face close to hers, and he had kissed her hand—she could remember that!

Even though she felt weak and limp and somehow far away from everything that was happening, his lips had the power to thrill her, and she wanted to go on listening to him talking to her.

'He is alive, and we are together,' she thought.

Even if she was hurt and she could feel that her throat was swollen, that was of no consequence beside the fact that the *Duc* was safe.

Now she only hoped she was not disfigured, for she

wanted to look beautiful for him. With an effort, because she was still drowsy from the drug which the Doctor had given her, she put her hand up to her neck.

It was very tender and when she swallowed it hurt; but not as badly as it had done last night when the Doctor had made her swallow a potion that was extremely unpleasant to taste.

She felt someone coming to the bed-side and realised that she was not alone in the bed-room. Then she saw Marie looking down at her.

"You are awake, *Madame*," Marie said. "The Doctor told me I was to give you something to drink when you awoke, which will ease the pain in your throat."

She did not wait for Syrilla to answer her but produced a glass, and putting her arms round her mistress's shoulders she raised her a little so that she could drink.

Whatever it was, it certainly did not taste as unpleasant as the drink she had been given the night before.

Syrilla thought she could recognise honey and glycerine and remembered her mother giving them to her when as a child she developed a sore throat.

Marie laid her back tenderly against the pillows and asked:

"Is there anything you would like me to do for you, *Madame?* Don't try to speak, but point and I'll understand."

Syrilla pointed to the curtains and Marie pulled them back. Now the sunshine came flooding in and Syrilla looked round her.

It was the *Duc*'s room! She thought it was exactly the right background for him, and she was in his bed!

She felt a little thrill at the thought, then told herself it was only because he would have known she would not wish to sleep in the room where he had killed her attacker.

She was glad that Astrid was dead.

Now the *Duc* was safe and, thinking back, she knew how afraid she had been for him.

It seemed strange, Syrilla thought, that Astrid should have tried to strangle her and that she might have died the same way as Zivana.

The first crime had broken the *Duc*'s heart and had made him dedicate his life to the woman he had loved and whom he had gone on loving all through the years.

He would not have felt so strongly about her, and yet perhaps he would have minded a little if she had died at the hands of the man he loathed and who had threatened his own life.

Astrid was dead, Syrilla thought, but Zivana still lived.

She had deliberately tried not to think of the locked room upstairs. Because she had been so happy in the *Duc*'s company she had let it lie at the back of her mind and her thoughts had shied away from it.

But now it was impossible not to remember that Zivana still lived on in this house, because she still lived in the *Duc*'s mind.

His love was locked away with her somewhere in that precious Shrine which only he entered and which was sacred to him.

For the first time in her life, Syrilla knew the pains of jealousy—a jealousy which seemed to stab her like a dagger and was far more painful than the marks on her neck.

She wanted the *Duc*'s love. She wanted him to think of her as a woman who was desirable and who attracted him as Zivana had done.

She had imagined that she could be content with friendship, companionship, the privilege of worshipping him as she had done as a child. But it was not enough—not nearly enough!

The emotion she had felt as she rushed to defend

him against a murderer was the passionate response of a woman who loved him as a man, and as her husband.

'I want him!' Syrilla thought. 'I want him here beside me. I want to be his wife. I want him to kiss me and touch me.'

Then almost as if an angel barred the way with a flaming sword, she knew that what lay between them and what would always lie between them was his love for a woman who was dead—a woman whose relics lay locked away in the Château and with them his heart.

It seemed to Syrilla at that moment as if she went down into a very special hell of her own from which there was no respite.

She had known last night that she now loved the *Duc* quite differently from the way in which she had loved him before.

Now agonisingly it seemed as if her whole body burned for him and her whole being reached out towards him, longing for him, loving him so intensely that she felt it would be impossible to go on seeing him without confessing what she felt.

Perhaps after all it would be best to do what his mother wanted, and let him give her a child to carry on the title.

But even as she thought of it, her whole soul rebelled at the thought of his touching her when he wanted to touch another woman, of his kissing her when it would seem like dust and ashes on his lips, since he only wanted Zivana.

Zivana! Zivana!

The name seemed to haunt her until she could almost hear it spoken on the air and carried in on the wind.

She moved from side to side at the sheer intensity of her feeling, without realising she was doing so.

Now she heard Marie in a low voice say to someone at the door:

"I think *Madame* has a little fever, *Monsieur le Duc*."

Syrilla was still, then she felt her heart turn over in her breast. Her eyes opened and they seemed to be filled with sunshine to the man who came across the room towards her.

"You are awake!" he said needlessly, and as her hands went out to find his she managed to answer in a hoarse, croaking voice very unlike her own:

"I . . . I am . . . all . . . right."

"You can speak! Oh, Syrilla, you can speak!"

There was an expression of delight on the *Duc*'s face that was unmistakable, and Syrilla held on to him as if he was a life-line that was pulling her back to safety and security.

"I . . . I . . . am . . . all . . . right," she whispered, "and . . . you are . . . safe."

"I am absolutely safe," the *Duc* answered, "and now all that matters is that you should get well quickly."

"I . . . feel . . . well, now that . . . you are . . . with me," Syrilla managed to say.

Her heart was singing because of the look in his eyes.

Chapter Seven

"Please, *Monsieur,* let me get up. I feel quite well now," Syrilla pleaded.

The Doctor looked at her with a smile.

"Your mother-in-law, *Madame la Duchesse Douairière,* has already persuaded me against my better judgement to agree to her travelling to Aix-les-Bains, and now you are bullying me into taking risks concerning you."

"*Belle-mère* is going away?" Syrilla asked in surprise.

The Doctor nodded.

"The *Duchesse Douairière* is very much better than she has been for some time," he said. "I think it is as much psychological as physical because she is so happy in her son's marriage."

Syrilla did not reply and after a moment he went on:

"She is very anxious to take the cure at Aix-les-Bains, and I think that she also wishes to leave you two young people alone. She is therefore leaving tomorrow and if she takes the journey in very easy stages it should do her no harm."

"I am glad," Syrilla said.

She waited, her eyes on the Doctor, and after a moment he said:

"Very well, *Madame,* I suppose I must accede to your request. You may get up and go downstairs for an early dinner, but afterwards you are to come straight back to bed, and rest tomorrow until I have seen you. Is that ageed?"

"Yes . . . I agree."

There was a lilt in Syrilla's voice and a light in her eyes which the Doctor did not miss.

"You have been through a very unpleasant experience," he said, "but you are young, *Madame,* and have great courage. I think it will do you no permanent harm."

When he left her Syrilla sat up in bed, planning what she would wear this evening for dinner with the *Duc*.

For two days the Doctor and the *Duc* had insisted that she must stay in bed, and in fact the first day after what she had suffered at Astrid's hands she did feel dizzy and her throat throbbed almost intolerably.

But now it no longer hurt and, although the bruises had turned black and blue, she felt well in herself and only frustrated by the restrictions that were imposed upon her when she wanted so much to be with the *Duc*.

She knew at the back of her mind that she was afraid that being alone and having no-one with him, he might find the Château so dull that he would return to Paris.

She had the feeling, although he had not said so, that he would not ask her to go with him, and knowing what had happened in the past when he had been away for years, she felt apprehensive and worried.

It was not only this which made her long to see him with an overwhelming intensity which seemed to grow hour by hour.

Having discovered her new love for him, it was

hard to control her feelings when he came to her side to kiss her hand and ask how she was: he stayed, it seemed to her, so short a time.

It was difficult not to embarrass him by telling him how much she loved him, how she longed for him to put his arms round her.

How, she asked herself, could he have carried her from her own room to where she was now without her being aware of it?

Because the *Duc* thought she would not wish to return to her own bed-chamber so soon after a man had been killed there, she had been left in the *Chambre du Roi.*

Every time she looked round her it brought the *Duc* so vividly to her mind that it was almost as if he lay beside her and she could touch him.

Marie, who had come into the room after the Doctor had left, broke in on her thoughts.

"*Monsieur le Médecin* says that you may rise, *Madame,* and dine downstairs," she announced. "That's good news—very good news—but I think when he sees *Monsieur le Duc* he'll insist on dinner being early."

"I want it early," Syrilla replied.

As far as she was concerned, the earlier the better, for then she could be with the *Duc* again.

She could look at him, listen to him, and perhaps whatever the Doctor said they would be able to sit alone for a little while in the Salon when dinner was finished.

"What will you wear, *Madame?*" Marie asked, and that of course was an absorbing subject which took them a long time to decide.

Syrilla discarded one gown after another, and when at length she had had her scented bath and was dressed, she wondered at the last moment if one of her other gowns would have been a better choice.

But in fact the gown she wore could not have been more becoming.

Of pink tulle, made with the skill that could only have come from Paris, the full skirt billowed out from her tiny waist and the tight bodice revealed the curves of her breasts.

There was a lace bertha embroidered with tiny stars which twinkled with diamanté, a draped skirt that was caught up with constellations of stars, and there was a cluster of them on each of her small satin shoes.

"*C'est ravissante, Madame!*" Marie exclaimed. "It's the most beautiful gown I've ever seen!"

Syrilla smiled, at the same time, she was wondering whether the *Duc* would think it beautiful.

Having lived in Paris he must have seen women wearing so many fabulous and exciting gowns; they could never mean the same to him as they meant to her and to Marie, who had never travelled outside Touraine.

Her neck remained a problem.

The bruises were very prominent against her white skin, and she was afraid the *Duc* would think them ugly.

Also it would remind him of what she had suffered, and he would insist that she must return to bed as quickly as possible.

There were diamond and pearl necklaces in her jewel-box, some of which had been wedding presents, some of which belonged to the Savigne family. But she thought they were too heavy and also might draw attention to what she wished to conceal.

Instead she and Marie arranged a thin piece of tulle round her neck and fastened it on one side where the bruises were worst with two small white orchids which had been included in one of the vases of flowers which decorated her room.

The flowers gave her a very young, fresh look and she wore no jewellery. Her thin fingers were ornamented only with her wedding ring.

Syrilla took a last look at herself in the mirror, then turned towards the door.

"Tonight, *Madame,* I think perhaps you would like to sleep in your own bed-room?" Marie asked as she reached it.

Syrilla hesitated for a moment.

"Yes . . . that would be best. I am sure *Monsieur le Duc* wishes to return to his own bed."

She wondered for a moment if the ghost of Astrid would haunt her and whether she would relive that moment when she had seen his dark body descending outside the window and not known what it was.

Then she told herself it would be very stupid and ill-bred to be afraid. Besides, the *Duc* would be next door and if she called out to him she was certain he would hear her.

She felt herself quiver at the thought, then told herself that she would never call him unless it was really urgent. If he came to her only out of courtesy or consideration, it would be worse than if she faced her own fears alone.

She went slowly downstairs to find the *Duc* waiting for her in the Salon.

She saw as she walked towards him the glint of admiration in his eyes that she always looked for. Her heart was beating frantically and she felt a strange and wonderful excitement seep over her because they were alone.

"This will not prove too much for you?" he asked in a low voice.

"No, of course not!" she answered. "I wanted to get up yesterday, but the Doctor would not agree to it."

"He is being sensible on my instructions," the *Duc* said. "You must take things very easy for a few days."

"Yes, of course," Syrilla agreed.

She had the strange feeling that their lips were saying one thing while their thoughts were really quite different.

She could not explain it to herself, but she felt as if she vibrated to something the *Duc* was feeling which she could not understand, but yet it was very wonderful.

He gave her his arm and took her in to dinner.

While the servants were waiting on them, bringing them delicious dishes that were far too numerous for Syrilla, the *Duc* talked to her about the Estate, of his plans for the vineyards, and about the visit he had made that afternoon to Tauxise.

"They are happier?" Syrilla asked.

"Thanks to you I have never met a more happy and contented collection of people," he answered. "The men are working hard dragging up the old vines, the women were washing and sewing, and the children's faces were scrubbed so clean that they seemed to shine like copper pans."

Syrilla laughed.

"I am sure they resented that!"

"I promised that when you were well enough you would pay Tauxise a visit. They speak of you as if you were a Saint sent from Heaven to help them."

"They should not do that," Syrilla protested. "It made me feel embarrassed when the women knelt and touched my skirt."

"You performed a miracle," the *Duc* said, "and they will never forget it."

He paused, then added quietly:

"Neither shall I forget what you have done for our people."

She felt the colour come into her cheeks and her eyes fell before his. Then almost as if it was an effort the *Duc* talked of other things until dinner was finished.

They went back to the Salon, and now because she was afraid he would send her to bed Syrilla went to the open window to look out into the garden.

As it was so early, the sun was only just sinking in a blaze of crimson and gold behind the trees in the

Park and it was reflected in the lake, which was also gold, while the shadows on the lawn were purple.

It made such a beautiful picture that Syrilla drew in her breath.

"Could any place be as lovely as this?" she asked.

"That is what I have often thought myself," the *Duc* said, "but, Syrilla, I want to talk to you."

There was a note in his voice which made her turn round quickly and look at him apprehensively.

There was something solemn in the way he spoke and she had a sudden fear that he was about to tell her he was going away.

Because she was so nervous she clasped her hands together, and she knew the *Duc* was feeling for words.

After a moment he said:

"On the first night of our marriage, Syrilla, you told me that you had overheard two people saying I had a locked room in the Château."

He paused, and feeling he expected her to answer she said in a frightened little voice:

"Y-yes . . . I heard . . . that."

"You suggested, I remember, that it was a Shrine in which I had locked away my heart."

Again he looked at her and now it was impossible for Syrilla to say above a whisper:

"Yes . . . that is . . . what I . . . thought."

"I want you to come with me to that room," the *Duc* said, "and see what it contains. It is in fact a Shrine to my love."

Syrilla felt as if she had been turned to stone.

Instead of her heart beating excitedly, she thought it had suddenly become frozen and there was ice creeping into her veins, paralysing her to the point where it was hard to think.

She tried to speak, but no sound would come from between her lips.

"Will you come with me now?" the *Duc* asked gravely.

She nodded and they walked across the room side by side. He stopped only to pick up a key from the writing-desk as he passed it.

"What can this mean?" Syrilla asked herself frantically.

Why was he suddenly showing her the locked room which he had dedicated to Zivana's memory and which she had tried to forget ever since their marriage?

She thought with sudden terror that perhaps he was going to explain to her once again that Zivana meant everything to him and he could no longer bear her to be his wife.

'He means to get rid of me,' Syrilla thought, and felt as if a thousand knives cut her into pieces and the pain of it was almost unbearable.

They walked in silence up the Grand Staircase and then the *Duc* turned and led the way along the corridors towards a part of the Château which Syrilla had never seen because she had learnt that the rooms were not in use.

As they reached what she knew must be the end of the house, they climbed another staircase and she guessed they were going to one of the turrets.

When they reached the top there was a landing with one door, and Syrilla knew she was right. This was one of the large turrets, of which there were four, one at each corner of the Château.

The *Duc* handed her the key he held in his hand, then stood to one side.

She took it from him automatically and knowing what he now expected her to do she felt it was impossible to obey him.

All the jealousy she felt for the dead woman seemed to well over her in a flood-tide to leave her shaking and at the same time afraid as she had never been afraid before.

How could there be any chance of her competing

with a woman who had held a man's love for nine years after she was dead?

A woman who had become sacred and the symbol of everything that was desirable and perfect, and yet was lost?

But because Syrilla was incapable of expressing what she was feeling, because she felt as if she were only a puppet which must obey the *Duc,* she inserted the key in the lock.

Although it looked heavy it turned easily, as if it had recently been oiled.

Just for a moment Syrilla hesitated. Then as the *Duc* did not move she pushed the door open.

At first glance she was surprised that the turret-room was so large. The floor was carpeted and the sun-light was coming in through the open windows. But that was not the only light in the room.

There were candles, large candles in gold candle-sticks, burning on either side of a picture and sur-rounded on both sides by flowers.

They were white and Syrilla could smell the fra-grance of lilies, roses, and carnations as she moved slowly towards the end of the room, feeling as if her feet were weighted down with lead.

But the picture on which the candlelight shone was not, as she expected, that of a stranger. It was a portrait of herself!

She recognised it instantly, for it was the one which her father had always liked of her and which he had presented to the *Duc* on their marriage.

She stared at it in bewilderment. Then with her eyes wide and a little frightened she turned to look at the *Duc*.

He was standing just a step behind her and he said:

"You wished to see what was enshrined in my heart."

For a moment Syrilla did not understand. Then as the ice within her breasts seemed to melt and a strange and wonderful feeling crept over her, the *Duc* said abruptly in a voice that was surprisingly harsh:

"I have a great deal to tell you, Syrilla. Sit down."

She looked at him in perplexity and she saw a damask-covered chair near her and sat down feeling as if her legs no longer carried her.

Her mind was in a turmoil, and yet because of what the *Duc* had said and because her protrait was the only object in the room she felt as if her eyes were blinded by the candlelight and there were the strains of music sounding in her ears.

The *Duc* walked to the open window to lean against it.

"You heard a story on the day of our marriage," he began, "that I had loved a ballerina called Zivana Mezlanski, and that when she was strangled I had all her belongings brought here to set them up in a Shrine to her memory."

He did not look at Syrilla as he spoke but at her portrait surrounded by candles and flowers.

He seemed to be waiting for her to speak and after a moment she said:

"I told . . . you that was . . . what I . . . heard."

"It was true," the *Duc* said. "I was twenty-one when I met Zivana and I thought she was the most exquisite dancer and the most beautiful person I had ever seen."

His lips tightened for a moment as he said:

"I fell in love with her—or rather I was infatuated, as only a young, idealistic man could be—with a woman from a very different world from the one in which he had always lived."

Syrilla clasped her hands together.

There was a pain in his voice as he spoke which was echoed in herself.

"I had known few women intimately before I met Zivana and certainly no women who lived the life she did. I thought she was so perfect, in every way, that I wanted to make her my wife."

He drew in his breath.

"I wanted her to marry me immediately and come back here to live with me at Savigne."

Syrilla wondered why he was telling her this. She knew it was hurting him to speak of the past and she tried not to think of her feelings, but of his.

"Zivana made many excuses why we would not be married at once," the *Duc* went on, "and she became my mistress, although in reality I felt it was a sacrilege against the greatness and sanctity of our love."

He paused before he added almost violently:

"I was a fool, Syrilla, an ignorant young fool who knew nothing about the realities of life!"

His voice seemed to echo round the room, before with an effort he went on in a quieter tone:

"Zivana put me off with promises—she would marry me when she had finished her contract at the theatre—when she had had just one more Season with the Ballet. It was excuses, always excuses, and I accepted them because there was nothing else I could do."

The *Duc* was silent for a moment. Then he said:

"How was I to know they were all lies? Lies that I was gullible enough to believe without question!"

Syrilla made a little gesture as if she wished to comfort him, but he continued:

"You know what happened. She was strangled by Jules Astrid, and I found her lying dead on the floor of her dressing-room."

"It . . . must have been a . . . terrible . . . shock," Syrilla whispered.

"I think I became a little insane," the *Duc* replied, "because I believed that if I had not been delayed in leaving the Auditorium after her performance I might have reached her dressing-room earlier and therefore saved her from her assailant's hands."

"You . . . knew who had . . . killed her?"

"One of the other performers had seen Astrid leaving Zivana's dressing-room," the *Duc* replied, "and when he subsequently disappeared it was obvious who her murderer had been."

"But they . . . caught . . . him?"

"Not for six months," the *Duc* answered. "During that six months I mourned Zivana as the woman who would have been my wife."

The *Duc* had not looked at Syrilla since he had started to speak and she thought it was because he could not bear to think of her taking the place of Zivana, whom he had loved with all his heart.

"Then Astrid was caught," the *Duc* went on.

Now he spoke quickly as if he wished to come to the end of his story.

"He was brought to Trial and it was then that I learnt the truth."

"The . . . truth?" Syrilla asked wonderingly.

"He had been Zivana's lover and it was he she cared for—not me!"

"Oh . . . no!" Syrilla whispered almost beneath her breath.

"Her letters to him were read out in Court," the *Duc* continued. "They revealed that the Zivana I imagined I knew had never existed. She was a wild, uncivilised Russian obsessed by a man because he was rough and brutal, a man who treated all women as chattels and had no use for them except physically."

There was so much bitterness in the *Duc*'s voice that Syrilla felt it was almost unbearable to listen to him.

She did not know that he was hearing again the letters that had been read out in Court as an extenuating reason for Astrid's crime.

Letters so passionate, so burning with violence and desire, that they held everyone in the Courtroom spellbound while the *Duc* had felt humiliated into the dust.

Zivana had even referred to him in her outpourings.

"Aristide is very young and knows nothing about love," she had written almost contemptuously, *"but he*

is rich and we need the money. But, oh, the agonies of being with him when I might be with you! I lie in his arms wondering who you are with, and I want you and need you, my whole body yearns and burns for you."

There had been dozens of letters written frantically by a woman who loved a man with a deep-seated Slavonic passion which made her veer between deep depression and a wild exhilaration.

The letters had revealed that Astrid had beaten her and knocked her about because he was jealous and that she had gloried in his brutality.

She loved him; at the same time, as she said over and over again, the *Duc* was rich and they both needed everything she could extract from him.

But money had not assuaged Astrid's jealousy.

In a fit of rage, when they must have quarrelled over the fact that she had another lover besides himself, he had strangled her.

The case had taken days while the *Duc* had passed through an indescribable hell.

When the verdict was brought in as a *Crime Passionell* he had changed from an idealistic youth to a man so cynical and bitter that there was nothing but hatred left in his heart.

Now he turned his back on Syrilla and stood looking out the turret window with unseeing eyes.

"I am not going to tell you of my life in Paris during the last eight years," he said. "You would not understand and, God knows, I have no wish for you to do so."

He paused for a moment.

"But I want you to realise that I was far from doing the noble work you envisaged. Instead I was committing every crime against decency that it is possible to imagine. I had been hurt and I wanted to hurt."

His lips tightened before he said:

"With every woman I met I tried to avenge myself

on Zivana. I hated them, and yet I used them for my own needs. If I ruined their lives or left them weeping and unhappy, it pleased me. Because I had been wounded and scarred—or so I believed—I wanted to crucify them!"

The hurt in his voice was very obvious and Syrilla was more aware of that than of the words he spoke.

"The way I behaved was a disgrace to my name and the traditions of my family," the *Duc* went on. "People remonstrated with me, but I laughed at them."

He drew in his breath before he said:

"No-one will have told you the truth, Syrilla, but I have become a by-word for all that is low and bestial—a man who is utterly debauched—a man who has dragged a noble title into the gutter and smeared it with mud."

There was so much self-condemnation in the way he spoke that Syrilla felt the tears come into her eyes.

He obviously did not expect her to answer him and after a second's silence, he said:

"When my mother asked me to marry for the sake of the continuity of the family, I told her I would have no part in choosing my bride. I meant to stay here one night and one night only, and then return to the gutters from which I had come."

Now Syrilla found her voice.

"Then . . . why did . . . you not do . . . so?"

"Because you were different from everything I had imagined still existed in the world," he answered. "Because you believed in me, because you brought back dreams that I thought I had lost nine years ago. Dreams of a woman who could be innocent and pure and inspire a man spiritually as well as physically."

"And then . . . ?" Syrilla asked.

"I fell in love with you!" the *Duc* replied. "I fought against it, make no mistake about that! I fought against everything you stood for, everything you are; but when I saw you struggling with Astrid, when I carried you in my arms and thought you were dead, I knew that I had lost my heart completely and irretrievably as I have never lost it before."

His voice deepened as he continued:

"I knew then that what I had felt for Zivana was the infatuation of a youth who had no knowledge of life and little sense of values. What I feel for you, Syrilla, is very different. I love you as a man, with my heart and with my mind, and, if I had one, which I doubt, my soul."

He made a gesture with his hand.

"You fill my whole life to the exclusion of all else. You are everything that is perfect. But I know only too well that I am utterly unworthy of you."

Syrilla made a little sound but it did not interrupt him.

"After the despicable manner in which I have behaved these last years, I am not certain if there is a way back even for a 'sinner who repenteth.' "

There was a passion in his words as he continued:

"I want you, Syrilla, I want you unbearably as my wife—my real wife. But what have I to offer you? I am certainly not the Knight you believe me to be, the hero who has no existence except in your imagination!"

The *Duc* paused, then he said cynically:

"I am not even certain that the love I have for you is clean, knowing the foul creature I have become!"

He drew in his breath, before he said almost as if it was a challenge:

"The answer is up to you. If you will take me as I am, I swear I will try to become what you want me to be. But I will not lie to you—I do not wish you to have any illusions about me! If you behave as you should, you will shrink away from me as something beyond the pale—a man with whom you could have nothing in common. The choice is yours."

The *Duc*'s voice seemed to die away and there was a silence in the room.

It was a silence so intense that Syrilla felt as if she was no longer breathing and the *Duc* too seemed to be holding his breath. Then suddenly she was at his side.

Without turning he heard a little voice say:

"Will you . . . tell me why . . . after we were . . . married . . . even though I told you what I felt . . . you did not make me your . . . wife as you . . . intended?"

"That is what I meant to do," the *Duc* replied, "but the first night I was too surprised by what you told me to have words in which to answer you. The second night when I came to your room you were praying, and I knew I could not spoil or hurt anything so pure and —perfect."

He heard Syrilla draw in her breath. Then she said:

"That was exactly how the . . . Knight in whom I believed would have . . . behaved . . . but just as you have changed and you say your . . . love for me is . . . different from anything you have ever felt before . . . so too is mine."

The *Duc* was listening intently, but he did not speak and after a moment she said very softly:

"I love you now not as my *Monseigneur*, not as someone dedicated to an ideal, but as a man! I love you, Aristide, and I long to be your . . . wife—your real wife . . . if you want me."

The *Duc* turned from the window.

"Want you?" he asked. "God knows I want you! But have you thought, Syrilla, about all I have told you?"

"Why should I think about it?" she asked. "To me you have always been everything that is . . . noble and fine. What happened in the . . . past does not concern . . . me. I want to be part of your . . . future . . . a future in which if you . . . love me as I love you we can be . . . together . . . here at . . . Savigne."

She saw the *Duc*'s eyes light up, and although he did not move or touch her she felt as if he drew nearer to her.

"Do you understand what you are saying?" he asked. "I love you, Syrilla, I love you as I swear I have never loved anyone before in the whole of my life! But you will have to teach me to find again all the things in which you believe and which once very long ago were mine."

There was something almost pathetic as he added:

"I have lost them and without them I am afraid that I shall not make you happy."

"All I . . . want is . . . you."

Now as if she could not help herself Syrilla put out her arms and as she did so the *Duc* pulled her almost roughly against him and looked down at her face raised to his.

"I love you! I adore you! I worship you!" he said. "Help me, Syrilla, to change myself back to the man you have believed in all these years but who is not worthy even to kiss the ground on which you stand."

"You are . . . everything I ever . . . dreamed of . . . or wanted," Syrilla whispered.

The *Duc* drew her closer, then almost as if he was afraid to touch her his lips sought hers.

It was a very gentle kiss—the kiss of a man who is pulsatingly aware of something sacred and approaches it with reverence.

Then as their lips met the wonder of it seemed to Syrilla to envelop them both with a blinding light that came not from the sky but from within their own hearts.

She felt herself draw closer and closer to the *Duc* and her body melted against his until they were no longer two people but one.

She felt her lips respond to the insistence of his, and a flame flickered within her which seemed to run through her veins with an ecstasy and a glory beyond anything she had ever dreamt of or imagined.

"I love you! I love you!" she wanted to say, but it was impossible to speak.

She only knew the *Duc* held her captive and at the same time it was as if in his kiss he dedicated himself, knowing that he asked from her that which she could only give in love.

When finally he raised his head to look down at her shining eyes, her cheeks flushed with happiness and her breath coming quickly from between her lips, he made a sound that was half an exclamation of triumph, and yet also a groan of contrition.

"You are so beautiful, my precious darling, so perfect in every way," he said. "I have told you that I am not worthy of you, and yet I love you so completely, so absolutely, that I cannot ever let you go."

"I have . . . belonged to you . . . already for . . . nine years."

"Why did I not know? Why did I not feel your love reaching out to save me from myself?"

"Perhaps because . . . you have . . . suffered, our love will seem more . . . precious and more . . . wonderful."

His arms tightened about her.

"I might have lost you!" he said. "If that fiend had killed you as he tried to do, there would be nothing left for me but to die in degradation and as quickly as possible."

"You were not meant to . . . die any more than I . . . was," Syrilla answered. "I think because . . . there is so much for you to do. You are . . . wanted here. Your people need you. I . . . need you! I want to be with you . . . always and . . . forever!"

"That is what we will be," the *Duc* promised. "But, oh, my darling little love, you must help me so that the crimes I have committed can be forgotten and people will once more respect the name of Savigne because you adorn it."

"We will do all that is . . . expected of us . . . together," Syrilla said, "but you do love me . . . you really do love me?"

It was the cry of a child who wants to be reassured and the *Duc* kissed first her forehead, then both of her eyes, before he said:

"It will take me a lifetime to tell you how much I adore you and to make you as happy as I mean to do. But now, my precious lovely one, you must obey the Doctor's instructions and go to bed."

"I . . . want to . . . stay with you. . . . I cannot . . . leave you," Syrilla whispered.

The *Duc* smiled and his lips were very close to hers as he asked:

"Who said anything about my leaving you?"

Syrilla felt her heart leap. Then almost as if she was afraid she had not heard him aright she whispered:

"You mean . . . ?"

"I mean that you are my wife," the *Duc* said, "and, my sweetheart, there will be no more barriers, no more secrets, no love locked in. We will be together as we were meant to be since the beginning of time, and I will teach you to love me as I love you."

"That is . . . what I . . . want," Syrilla murmured. "That, my darling, wonderful Aristide, is what I have been . . . praying for."

"Then why are we waiting?" the *Duc* asked.

He picked her up in his arms as he spoke.

With his lips holding hers completely captive, he carried her close against his heart down the stairs from the turret, leaving the door wide open behind them.

About the Author

Barbara Cartland, the celebrated romantic novelist, historian, playwright, lecturer, political speaker, and television personality, has now written over two hundred books. She has had a number of historical books published and several biographical ones, including a biography of her brother, Major Ronald Cartland, who was the first Member of Parliament to be killed in the war. The book has a preface by Sir Winston Churchill.

In private life Barbara Cartland is a Dame of Grace of St. John of Jerusalem and one of the first women, after a thousand years, to be admitted to the Chapter General.

She has fought for better conditions and salaries for midwives and nurses, and, as President of the Hertfordshire Branch of the Royal College of Midwives, she has been invested with the first Badge of Office ever given in Great Britain, which was subscribed to by the midwives themselves.

Barbara Cartland has also championed the cause of old people and founded the first Romany Gypsy Camp in the world. It was christened "Barbaraville" by the gypsies.

Barbara Cartland is deeply interested in Vitamin Therapy and is President of the National Association for Health.